Weary, Come Home

Weary, Come Home
Copyright © 2021
Abby Rosser

ISBN: 978-1-952474-68-2

Cover concept and design by David Warren.

Published by WordCrafts Press
Cody, Wyoming 82414
www.wordcrafts.net

Weary,
Come Home

a novel

ABBY ROSSER

WordCrafts Press

Prologue

Heidi veered slowly into the driveway, unconsciously pacing her rental car's acceleration to the slow clicking of her turning signal. She was experiencing an inward struggle. It was as if her right hand was pulling the steering wheel to turn toward the squatty blue ranch house, and her left hand was trying pull the other way, toward anywhere but the little rambler situated at 374 Verbena Drive. In the end, her right hand won.

After she was safely under the shaded carport, Heidi shut off the engine. She sat in the muffled quiet of the rental car and listened. The muted sounds of traffic, suburban wildlife, and the man mowing next door made her feel suddenly and completely exhausted. More than thirty hours of solo driving will do that to you. What was she thinking, driving all the way here from L.A.? She checked her phone—three voicemail messages from her agent, Beverly. Heidi shut it off and placed the phone in her Gucci handbag. She brushed her hand along the colorful embroidery on the front of the purse—a pair of the ugliest pug dogs anyone had ever sewn on Italian leather. She questioned why she had spent so much money on something she never really liked in the first place.

Get out of the car, she told herself. *Imagine that this is an improv skit, and you're someone else. Or turn the car back on and drive to McDonald's. You know you've been craving one of those disgusting Filet-O-Fish sandwiches Poppy liked to get for you. Just do something because you came all this way, and now you're about to pee your pants.* She inhaled as if she were filling up her lungs before diving underwater and opened the car door.

Walking up the steps to the front door, Heidi felt a rush of familiarity mixed with a sliver of disappointment that the scene didn't flawlessly match her memory. The flower beds separating the house from the sidewalk were overgrown with spurge, thistles, and wild onions. A shutter was missing from one of the front windows. She noticed flecks of black paint peppered across her palms after she lifted her hands from the metal railing running alongside the crumbling steps.

She slid her sunglasses on top of her head and squared her shoulders. As she was about to ring the doorbell, Heidi noticed that the front door was partly opened. She pushed lightly and opened it just in time to hear an enraged cry. "Get outta my house, you winged demon!" The scream was followed by the sound of glass breaking. Heidi fumbled in her purse, searching for her phone so she could call 911. But before she could dial the number, something flew toward her.

Heidi screeched and dropped to the ground. She flattened herself on the top step, clutching her purse with one arm and covering her head with the other. A whooshing sound passed over her. She opened one eye just enough to see a pair of fuzzy blue slippers and rolls of knee high panty hose piled up around two puffy, spider-veined ankles. Heidi lifted her head to take in the rest of the short, round figure standing defiantly in front of her: a pink and purple floral housecoat with half of the snaps unfastened and two jiggly, liver-spotted arms clutching a broom and shaking it towards the sky. "And don't you come back, you filthy vulture!"

"Mo?" Heidi squeaked out.

For the first time, the old woman noticed the crumpled form on her stoop. "Heidi? Doll Baby! But what in heaven's name are you doing down there? Come on inside, honey!"

Heidi stood and brushed the dust off her blue jeans. Spying the sunglasses which had fallen off her head and were now lying next to her foot, she bent down to pick them up, silently groaning at the broken, twisted, designer wreckage and gloomily slid them in her purse. She followed the woman inside the house.

As they walked through the living room and into the kitchen, the woman ranted, "Those swifts keep getting in the house, flying down my chimney—ugly, screechy things. The damper's busted so I can't shut the flue, and those dummies just come right in, like they were invited to Sunday supper. I can't stand 'em." She hung the broom on a hook on the far side of the kitchen, next to the back door. "I know we're s'posed to love all God's creatures, but those birds just don't do anything for me. Now, give me a fine-looking cardinal or one of those cute, little chickadees…" The woman began without finishing her sentence. Then she motioned to one of the polished cherry, high-backed chairs tucked into the dining table. "Sit down and tell me what you've been doing lately, Doll Baby. Then, once I catch my breath, I'm gonna make you something good to eat. You're skinny as a string bean."

"Oh, I wouldn't want you to go to any trouble, Mo," said Heidi, as she pulled out the chair for the elderly woman to sit down.

"Trouble? It's never trouble to do something for my granddaughter! You're about the only kin I got left, Heidi Seek."

Heidi winced slightly hearing her name. "You know, I don't go by Heidi Seek anymore. Once I got to Hollywood, I changed my name to Heidi Phillips…after Daddy."

Mo reached across the table and patted her granddaughter's hand. "And he would've loved that, I'm sure. Your Mama said you thought Heidi Seek sounded like a name for one of those sinful dancers who spin 'round on poles, wearing only their drawers."

"Beverly, my agent, thought it would be better to change it," Heidi explained. "They call it branding."

"I don't know anything about branding, and come to think of it, I don't know much about naming, either. Other than your daddy and an imaginary friend who lived under our porch that I called Mrs. Chumley, I don't recall ever naming anything else, and I didn't even come up with your daddy's name by myself. When he was born, me and your Poppy 'bout had a fit agreeing on a name for him. Poppy wanted to name him James—Poppy came from a long line of Jameses which is why he had to go by Jimbo—but I wanted my baby to have something all his own. I made a list of names based on things

I liked while I was pregnant with him: *Chip, Berry, Ritz*—that one sounded so fancy, and those crackers were about all I could stomach for the first few months of my pregnancy. I also wrote down *Harvey*—that was the name of my favorite department store…such pretty Christmas decorations, even had a talking Christmas tree. We finally made a compromise with Phillip. It felt safe to pick a Bible name. Did you know Phillip means *lover of horses*? I don't reckon he ever sat on any horse, but he did try to sit on a neighbor's goat once. He ended up with a sore be-hind. Still, he always wanted to bring that old goat any kitchen scraps I had lying around. Do you think there's a name that means *lover of goats*?"

"Not that I know of," Heidi answered. "I don't think you ever told me where *your* name came from. Why does everyone call you Mo?"

"That's quite a tale to tell, honey." Mo reached down and pulled up her stockings. "These Underalls are s'posed to be good for my cir-cul-ation, but I doubt they got any elastic left in 'em." She picked up a church bulletin from the table and began to fan herself with it. "I'll have to travel back near eighty years to answer that, but if you're willing to listen, I'm willing to talk."

Morgan's Hat, Tennessee, 1941

Pastor Cooley couldn't remember the last time he had seen the top of his desk. He had a vague memory of a ink blotter calendar advertising the *H. H. Jarvis Federal Savings & Loan* and the year *1920* inscribed at the top, and he assumed it must still be there somewhere, under all this jumble of scholarly debris. His secretary, the industrious middle-aged widow Tillie Bransford, had received the calendar from her bank. Within a week of the untimely death of her husband Elmer, Tillie had moved to Morgan's Hat, found a job at Berea Baptist Church, and opened a new bank account. She was given a choice between the calendar and a tin coin bank with a comic strip character painted on the side and a word bubble saying, "A penny saved is a penny earned." She decided the calendar was more practical.

Pastor Cooley had never had a secretary before Tillie came, though he had been at this post since 1909. Tillie had remarked on her first day that this was evident. She had cleared away the cups stained by coffee sediment or tobacco juice still lingering at the bottom, re-shelved the stacks of books with a methodical system of her own design, filed any important documents in the filing cabinet and burned the unnecessary ones in the church furnace. She had placed the calendar on the empty desk, recommending that the pastor use it to plan out his sermons.

But that must've been close to twenty years ago. Tillie had eventually admitted her defeat and ceased entering his tiny office, letting

Pastor Cooley know that he was welcome to join her in the outer office to discuss any church matters requiring her attention, but she was unable to step inside his office for the reason that doing so would force her to leave work early and head home with a sick headache.

Pastor Cooley had to admit he was a little afraid of Tillie at first. Her neatness, efficiency, and foresight which bordered on mind-reading was a mystery to him and a bit unnerving. Growing up the youngest of eighteen children, Zeal Cooley was accustomed to disorganization to the overall degree of general raggedness. To that point, it wasn't until after he had completed seminary school that he had owned anything brand new. To celebrate his graduation, he had bought himself a new pair of wool trousers and was thrilled how well they fit his petite five-and-a-half foot frame. He later felt compelled to repent of such a deep love for a material possession and put the trousers in the missionary barrel which contained clothing sent to foreign lands for those less fortunate.

Secondhand and well-worn items were not only customary for the Cooley household, Zeal had come to the conclusion that it would be the ultimate preference for Jesus Christ himself—the Messiah who, unlike the foxes with their dens and the birds with their nests, had no place to lay his head—to live in much the same way the Cooley clan did. Considering that he was a confirmed bachelor, Zeal wasn't overly concerned with tidiness, let alone home décor and social entertaining. His house was simple and practical. No frills or fripperies.

Two decades had passed since Tillie had first introduced the significance of office organization, and though her instructions had originally fallen on the uninterested ear of Pastor Zeal Cooley, today somehow felt different. As he sat at his desk staring at the mounds of papers, books, and dirty dishes in front of him, Zeal decided to clean.

He gathered the trash from the top of his desk, under his desk, piled in the chairs opposite his desk and on the floor, and he placed it all into a wire wastebasket. Then he carried the overflowing bin out the door. "I'm just going round the back to the furnace, Mrs. Bransford," Zeal called to Tillie as he strode past her desk where she sat just beyond the door to his private office. She nodded her head but didn't speak to him. He noticed she held the phone to her ear, no doubt listening to the woes and grumbles of one of their church-going saints. Zeal silently said a prayer of thanksgiving for his secretary who spared him from many of these conversations. He heard her say in commiseration, "Well, bless your heart," just as he walked out.

The doorway to the modest church offices stood to the left of the pulpit in the sanctuary. To get to the basement furnace, a person had to step outside using the exterior door to the right of the pulpit, head down the stairs and around to the back, and then walk down another set of stairs. As he passed the raised pulpit, absorbing the sunlight streaming through the tall, arched windows flanking either side of the narrow room, he paused. Zeal loved the hushed quiet of the empty room, and he often sat there alone in the middle of the day to pray for his flock. But an unseen force was urging him to continue on his journey.

He opened the door and nearly tripped over something on the top step. Zeal set his wastebasket aside and knelt to examine a large, wooden crate. On the side of the wooden slats was a brightly colored picture—an apple painted in the center of an orange pyramid which seemed to be floating atop a brilliant blue river. PHARAOH ORCHARDS OF MEMPHIS was written in bold red letters across the top. Inside the crate, Zeal saw only a knitted blanket of pale pink yarn which he assumed was a donation for the missionary barrel. Then Zeal saw something moving amidst the blankets. A tiny hand emerged with five tiny fingers stretching then curling into a fist. The fist ferreted in the folds of the blanket until they parted to reveal a tiny face, where the fist found a home in one of the smallest mouths Zeal had ever seen. The gray-blue eyes of the tiny face opened and regarded the old bachelor, then the mouth let out a teeny coo like the sound of a contented dove.

Carefully, Zeal lifted the crate and looked in the direction of the wooded area around the side door of the church. He nearly called out, shouting "Anybody there?" But he decided against it lest the noise upset the baby. He carried the crate inside, past the pulpit and into the office. Setting the wooden box on Tillie's desk, Zeal waited for her to finish her phone call.

"That was Nadine Henderson," she told Zeal once she had said goodbye. Tillie was refastening the clip-on earring which resembled a cluster of purple grapes back on her right ear. She used both hands to smooth her hair in the front and repositioned a hair pin at the top of her head to keep an impressive wave of brown hair in place. "Her son has taken up drinking again. So sad. I told her you'd be by tomorrow afternoon." Tillie wrote the appointment in her date book and turned her plump face toward Zeal. She shifted her glasses with their thick, purple frames and the tiny silver stars in the corners so she could look inside the crate. "Now what do we have here, Pastor? A donation for the less fortunate?"

Zeal reached inside the crate and lifted the baby out. "I believe it's a baby, Mrs. Bransford."

"A baby?" Tillie stood up quickly. "Lands sake! Why didn't you say so right away! Oh! It's a bitty thing."

"Do you recognize it? Is it familiar to you?" asked Zeal, cradling the child in the crook of his arm.

"I don't think so."

"I've seen many infants in my time, and one baby looks as much like another to me."

Tillie was rooting around in the crate, looking for any clues to the child's identity. She removed an envelope with a single word neatly printed on the front: *Pastor*. "Alright if I open it?" she asked. Zeal nodded and she pulled out a piece of sheet music. She flipped it over and read the neat cursive:

Pastor Cooley,

I am too deep in shame to tell you who I am, but I have seen enough of your goodness to know that you help people and I need your help. This is my baby girl. I am not able to care for her anymore as I must now travel for work. I had hoped to find a different occupation with easier hours, but the only thing I know how to do is to be a musician. It is a difficult job for a woman but even more difficult for a woman with a baby. Years ago when I was a young girl visiting family, I heard you preach a sermon about the woman who bathed Jesus' feet. I have never forgotten it. Just as Jesus was merciful to her, I know you will not judge me too harshly. Please raise her so that she will always know she is loved.

Gratefully,

A

Tillie plopped down in her chair. "Have you ever heard anything so desperately sorrowful?" She removed a white handkerchief from one of her desk drawers and dabbed her eyes. "It's enough to break a person's heart." Zeal had been staring at the baby girl's gray-blue eyes while Tillie read the letter. He felt as if he were locked into her gaze, unable to move or speak or even blink. "Pastor?" Tillie attempted to break him from the spell. "Pastor, what are you going to do?"

"Do?" he asked as if in a daze.

"Yes. What are you going to do about the baby? Should I call the sheriff?"

Zeal swallowed hard. "I—I reckon it has to be done. It's only right that the Law decide these cases." He glanced up and saw that Tillie was watching him with that deliberate, practiced stare of hers. He could almost feel her unraveling his thoughts, untangling them so that she could tell him what to do.

"Would you like to name the child first?" she asked. "It seems un-Christian to just call her *the baby*. Maybe you could name her after your mother—wasn't her name Edna-Jean? Or you could pick a Bible name—Esther or Ruth?"

Pastor Cooley glanced down at the picture on the fruit crate, then he lifted his chin and smiled. His brownish-gold eyes deepened to the color of an old penny, just as they did when he was delivering a particularly profound thought in one of his sermons. "As the Good Book says," he replied with confidence. "Her name shall be Moses for I drew her out of the Nile."

374 Verbena Drive

Heidi had listened to Mo's words with interest, but when her grandmother came to a break in her story, she was suddenly reminded of the many cups of coffee she had consumed on the long drive. "Is it alright if I use your bathroom?" Heidi asked.

"Why, of course, honey. You know where it is. Help yourself."

Heidi walked down the short carpeted hallway and turned left into the small bathroom. Everything was just as she remembered it—the powder blue tile which went halfway up the walls and covered the floor; the powder blue toilet, sink, and tub; the fuzzy pink bath mat and toilet seat cover; the shower curtain made from fabric featuring fat cabbage roses of light pink, mauve, and cream with a blue background; the wallpaper border along the top of the walls with a similar pattern of roses.

As she was finishing up in the bathroom and washing her hands, she pulled her long blonde hair into a loose bun on the top of her head. Then she examined her reflection in the mirror and frowned. She looked pale, and there were dark circles under her eyes. Looking away from the mirror, Heidi gazed out the little window to her left. A cream-colored, lacy curtain hid the top pane of glass, but she could still see a section of Mo's backyard in the lower pane. Craning her neck slightly, Heidi spied the weeping willow she vaguely remembered playing beneath when she was very small. Something about its limp branches made her feel sad. This melancholy feeling restarted the litany of critical self-attacks scrolling through her mind.

Ever since she had started her trip, Heidi had tried to ignore the questions popping into her head: Why wasn't she more excited about her new job, the thing she had wanted since she was old enough to know what an actor was? Why did she drive away from her West Hollywood apartment? Why did she leave the man who said he loved her without telling him where she was going? She silently shook her head.

Hanging from a hook in the ceiling was a macramé plant hanger, but instead of a plant, the pot held Mo's small assortment of beauty tools and makeup. Heidi smiled as she peered inside the pot to see tweezers, nail clippers, a compact, a few tubes of lipstick, denture cream, baby powder, and a pintail comb. She looked at the set of three drawers to the right of the sink and wondered why Mo didn't keep her things in there. Feeling a tiny spasm of guilt for being nosy, she slid open the top drawer. It was filled with rows and rows of medicine bottles. Heidi closed the drawer quickly, not caring to be reminded of her late grandfather's illness. She assumed the bottles had been prescribed for Mo's husband, Jimbo, years ago, when he was suffering from emphysema.

She opened the next one. It held Jimbo's aftershave lotion, razor, and hairbrush. Heidi ran her fingers across the rough bristles of the brush before shutting the drawer. The bottom drawer was stuck and would only open an inch. She sat down on the neon pink bath mat and put her hand inside the drawer, trying to push down the object which was preventing her from opening it. She felt a long, rounded piece of smooth plastic which she maneuvered side to side until it could lie down. Once she opened the drawer, she saw what her fingers had felt—a bubble bath bottle shaped like Bozo the Clown. She held it in her hand, staring at the spots where the red and blue paint had scratched off. Heidi set it aside and looked at the drawer's other contents. She saw plastic boats, a flattened tube of toothpaste, and a collection of moldy pennies.

Then she spied a leather grooming kit with the initials *P.S.* embossed in one corner. Heidi unzipped the case, finding only a glass bottle of Stetson cologne, half full of the yellow liquid. She unstoppered it and held the bottle to her nose. The smell instantly prompted her to think of her father. She conjured a hazy memory of him, young and alive and carrying her on his shoulders as she wrapped her arms around his neck and buried her face in his hair. It was a faraway memory, as accessible and frequently visited as the dusty corner of an unreasonably high kitchen cabinet. The memory held no sharply defined details such as time or place, and yet she could just summon it with the aid of the musky, cedar scent. She replaced the top of the cologne bottle and put everything back, making sure that Bozo was lying down so that she could close the drawer.

When she returned to the kitchen, Heidi found Mo sliding a grilled cheese sandwich on to a plate. "Sit down, Doll Baby, and eat this." Mo set the spatula she had used for the grilled cheese on a ceramic spoon rest which was in the shape of a horse's head decked out with a wreath of red roses around its neck. "And I've got half an apple pie in the fridge. You can eat some of that after you finish your sandwich."

Looking at the cheesy, golden sandwich, Heidi's first instinct was to mentally count the carbs and refuse the offered meal, but she was too overcome with a mixture of hunger and nostalgia to decline. "Thanks, Mo." She took a bite, enjoying the crispy, salty deliciousness while realizing how much she had missed eating plain old white bread and American cheese.

Mo stepped over to the refrigerator and opened the door. "Can I get you a glass of milk or some orange juice or maybe some iced tea?"

"I'll have some tea. Wait…is it made with sugar?"

Mo looked at her with a strange expression. "As opposed to what?"

"Oh, I don't know. I thought maybe you might use Splenda or agave nectar or something."

"You've been in California too long, honey." She placed several ice cubes in two tall drinking glasses, each one etched with a design of grapevines, and filled them with tea. Then she sat one of the glasses in front of Heidi and waited for her to take a sip. "Good, huh?" asked Mo after Heidi had swallowed a gulp of the sugary drink.

"Yes, ma'am."

Mo nodded her head with an air of satisfaction, as if she had unequivocally won a controversial argument. She sat down across from Heidi and sipped from her own glass.

Heidi took another bite of her sandwich and chewed thoughtfully for a moment before saying, "I hope you don't mind me asking, but why do you still have Daddy's things in that bottom drawer in the bathroom?"

Mo ran her finger along the line of grapevines on her glass, staring at the ice cubes bobbing up and down. "I'm not good at getting rid of things, I s'pose. Besides, the way I see it, those things aren't bothering anybody just sitting in those drawers. Truth is, I miss your Daddy and your Poppy, too."

"I could help you clean out the drawers, if you'd like," said Heidi. "Unless you don't want to. If it would be too painful, we could just leave them. Although, my yoga instructor always says, 'The fact that you refuse to do it means that you *must* do it.'"

Mo pulled her eyebrows down in a confused frown. "Well, I don't know what that means, but I do know that I have a hard time letting things go. Pauline, that's my cross-the-street neighbor, she says it's because I'm a Gemini, so I'm always going back and forth between the things I'm passionate about. She knows all about horoscopes and zodiac signs and such. I think she's tiptoeing in the devil's backyard with that nonsense, and I've told her as much, but I can see her point."

"Wait, how can you be a Gemini?" Heidi asked. "I thought you and Daddy had the same birthday. And he was born in January."

"Well, that's a funny story. You see, I don't actually remember when I was born—it just isn't a day I usually mark on the calendar. Though, if I recall correctly, it's sometime the middle of June, making me a Gemini. I only told your Daddy that we had the same birthday when he was little on account of him being so sad about the Bobbsey Twins."

"The Bobbsey Twins? You mean the books?"

"That's right. Those books were some of his favorites. He liked hearing about them going to the circus or playing in the snow or spending time on a houseboat. I'd read them to him at bedtime when he was young. He always wanted to have brothers and sisters, but, of course, he was an only child. So hearing about two sets of twins in one family…well, it nearly destroyed him. So one night, when he was feeling 'specially low, I told him that me and him were born on the same day only twenty-five years apart, so we were a kind of twins. That seemed to comfort him, for some reason. I s'pose I never told him otherwise."

"So, because you were left at the church in a fruit crate, you never knew for sure when you were born?"

"Yes, in a manner of speaking. Truth be told, I never celebrated the day I was born."

"That's so sad." Heidi frowned.

"No, not really. Other days just pushed in front of my birthday in the list of important days, I s'pose."

"Well, did you ever find out what happened to your mom?" Heidi asked. "Was she someone who lived in the town? Was she really a musician? Did the pastor raise you all by himself?"

"That's a lot of questions, Doll Baby. Lemme pick up the story after the fruit crate as it was told to me."

Morgan's Hat, Tennessee, 1941

Sheriff Isham Brown came by the church office and took a statement from Zeal about the baby girl. "So, you say you don't recognize the child or know about any expecting mothers in your congregation who might've left her?" Sheriff Brown asked as he looked at the note they had found within the folds of the blanket inside the crate.

"No, we were wholly perplexed by the appearance of the child," Zeal answered. He was bouncing the irritable baby and watching the door. Tillie had offered to run to Padgett's Grocery store to buy necessary items, such as bottles and diapers. He was anxious for her to return. He gave the baby his pinkie to suck on and swung her from his right hip then to his left, twisting at his waist.

Sheriff Brown watched the pastor intently, then he drew closer and lowered his voice to make a pointed suggestion, "You seem real comfortable with the little lady. You *sure* you don't know the mother?"

"What are you suggesting, Ish?"

"Well, things happen…even to church folk. It would explain her being dropped off here, especially to you, if you were the…well, you know…"

"The father?" Zeal responded in a shocked whisper. "Seeing as how I've known you all your life—baptizing you and marrying you to your lovely wife Hazel—you're just going to have to take me at my word when I say that this child is not of my loins. I don't know any more about this than what I've already told you."

"Alright, Pastor, alright. I'm sorry." Sheriff Brown removed his hat to scratch his head. "I didn't set out to offend you."

"I know you're just doing your job, but I want it understood here and now that this child is innocent of any immorality." The baby had fallen asleep in his arms and was contentedly sucking on one of her knuckles. "She will have a hard enough time growing up with the questionable circumstances of her birth, so we don't want to invite any rumors to chase after her all her days. As the Good Book says: 'Where there is no wood, the fire goes out; so where there is no gossip, the strife ceases.'"

"Yessir," Sheriff Brown answered meekly, eyes downcast, then he replaced his hat and attempted to resume a professional demeanor after being scolded. "Matt Watson's wife is due to give birth in a month or so. Maybe she could take the baby off your hands. It'd be just as easy to raise two babies at once, I reckon." Sheriff Brown stroked the baby's soft cheek. "Sure is a pretty, little thing."

"I've been given the task of caring for the child, so, with the help of the Lord, I will do my best. Unless you locate any of her kin, *I* will raise her."

"People in town will be expecting you to find a woman to do the raising. And since you're getting up in age, Pastor…"

"If I need help, you can be sure that I'll ask for it. I may be a 56-year old bachelor, plucked bald, with rheumatism in all my joints, but I've also been an uncle for all my life with more than fifty nieces and nephews. And though none of their babies were ever as tiny as this one, I don't need to go to all the trouble of getting a wife in order to take care of Moses."

"And you're sure about the name? That is, you don't want to think it over a bit?"

"I'm sure of it. But if it'll make you feel better, I'll come up with a more feminine middle name for her. Would that suit you?"

Tillie entered the office area carrying two overfilled paper bags. "I got everything on the list, Pastor," she said. "Oh, the little dear finally tuckered herself out." She set the bags on her desk and emptied them. "I would've been here earlier, but I took the bottles home to sterilize them. I boiled the water at my house. You know, you can't be too careful with babies! I mixed up several bottles, each with Carnation milk, clean water, and a tablespoon of Karo syrup."

Zeal watched Tillie organize piles of cloth diapers and baby gowns. As always, her tidying skills were on display and highly impressive. She handed him one of the bottles and directed him to sit in her chair—an identical wooden, swivel chair to the one in his office except that Tillie's chair had floral, pintucked cushions tied to the seat and back for added comfort. Moses stirred as soon as he sat down, but before she had a chance to cry, Zeal had the bottle in her mouth in one swift motion. She gulped down the bottle with vigor, then smiled a milky grin when it was drained empty.

"She is a tiny thing," said Tillie, as she watched Zeal expertly burp the satisfied baby by sitting her upright in his lap and firmly patting her back. "I don't suppose we could rightly guess her age."

"I've been studying on that," Zeal answered. "With her strong neck and the way she's sucking her knuckles and wearing that pie-eating grin, and…" He felt inside her mouth, "The fact that's she's all gums, I'd say she's round two or three months old. She's just on the small side of average."

"Well, someone's been caring for her proper," said Sheriff Brown. "That's plain to see, but I still need to make my inquiries. We don't approve of babies being left on doorsteps, as a rule." The sheriff hiked up his pants, tipped his hat, and said his good-byes.

Zeal laid the now-sleeping baby in the fruit crate still located on Tillie's desk. "Mrs. Bransford, I'd like you to make your own inquiries about Moses," he whispered. "Without giving too much away, ask the sisters in the Tuesday Sewing Circle if they've heard about a lady musician passing through town. Don't give the question too much weight. Just work it into regular conversation at Sullivan's Drug Store or the post office or Gordon's Hardware. You understand?"

Tillie tilted her head down and looked at Zeal over her glasses. She wore the smile of an indulgent aunt on the verge of pinching the cheek of her precocious nephew who presumed he knew better than his elders, then she smiled. "I understand 'xactly what you mean," she answered, confidently. "A woman can't hardly call herself a church secretary unless she's able to dish out enormous platefuls of discretion. This job requires a real sense of delicacy, and I've been doing it for over twenty years." She picked up her purple handbag, slipped it over her wrist and slid the handle down to the crook of her arm. "You just leave everything to me." Then Tillie left the office.

Though she was one of only a handful of women in Morgan's Hat who drove a car, Tillie walked past her prized Plymouth and in the direction of the town square. She slowed her walk to a stroll and smiled at an older couple walking towards her. "Afternoon, Deacon Foster…Miss Birdie." she said, cheerfully. "And how are all the Fosters?"

"Afternoon," the couple responded in unison.

"We're all fit as a fiddle," said the woman. "Just been visitin' with some church folks."

"Sure gettin' to feel like Fall," said the man before sneezing into his handkerchief. "My hay fever is right on schedule."

"Well, I hate to hear it," Tillie replied. "Ya'll get any news from your people in Nashville? Any big doings at the Capital? I hear your son Everette is doing good things as a state senator."

Tillie continued to chat with the Fosters, listening and responding to their stories about their children's and grandchildren's accomplishments. She filed away the anecdotes and continued to make her way around the square, stopping every once in a while to initiate small talk with another townsperson.

By the time Tillie arrived back at the church at 5:00, Sheriff Brown was chatting with Zeal as the pastor finished changing a wet diaper.

"No one I spoke to has any information about the baby or the mother," said the sheriff. "I talked to Doc Jameson. He said he didn't deliver the baby. He's going to ask around to doctors in surrounding counties and see if they know anything about it from about two months ago."

Zeal unrolled his sleeves and rebuttoned the cuffs. "I'm grateful for your inquiries into the matter." He wrapped Moses in a blanket and held her against his chest.

"I reckon I'll head home and see what Hazel's cooking for supper," Sheriff Brown said before he walked out the door.

"I thought he'd never leave," said Tillie once she heard the growling engine of the sheriff's truck. "Two months ago? Isham Brown really has no imagination! We have to go much further back to find this woman." She opened the top drawer of a filing cabinet and walked her fingers along the tabs.

"How do you figure?" asked Zeal.

"In the letter, the woman…let's call her Miss A, because of her initial at the end…said she heard you preach on the woman who washed Jesus' feet. You preached that sermon a few years after I came to work for you. I remember typing it up…your spelling is disgraceful, Pastor. You spelled *alabaster* with two bs and for *ointment* you put a *k* instead of a *t*. I remember because I made the joke that an *oink-mint* would be a piece of candy to eat after a plate of ribs. Ah! Here it is!" She lifted a sheet of paper from the back of the drawer. "May 14, 1922. 'Luke 7: The Sinful Woman'. This must've been the Sunday she came to church."

"Remarkable," said Zeal. "I couldn't tell you what I preached last week…"

"Seeing as how you haven't left the Old Testament in more than a decade, we're still suffering alongside the minor prophets," Tillie replied under her breath. "Of course, it's not my place to say so…"

"Pardon?" Zeal asked.

"Nothing, Pastor. Not a blessed thing." Tillie squealed in delight, as she shut the drawer and held the paper high above her head triumphantly. "My point is that Miss A came here as a child nineteen years ago."

"That could be just about anyone. How in heaven's name can we narrow down a list like that?"

"Well, I had a thought while I was out visiting downtown. We're looking for a woman who came here as a child—in my mind, she must've been between seven and ten years old when she heard your sermon, young enough to consider herself a young girl but old enough to remember the focus of a particular sermon. And she said she was staying with a family member, probably an aunt or grandmother, if I had to guess. Her letter had excellent penmanship and *spelling*…" Tillie smirked at Zeal reproachfully before continuing, "which makes me believe she was educated past grammar school, most likely attending some sort of music school. So we're looking for a woman in her late 20s with an educated background who had a relative living in Morgan's Hat."

"I still don't know…"

"Family loves to brag on family, Pastor," Tillie interrupted. She took out a compact from her purse and reapplied her lipstick as she looked in the small mirror. "As long as you don't need me to help out with the baby, I'll skedaddle."

"I believe I can handle things with Moses alright, but what are you going to do?"

"I'm going to pay a call on a few folks after supper." She snapped the compact closed and smiled. "And there should be a crib on your front porch when you get home. I got it and a few other sundry things donated for the baby. 'Night, Pastor!"

374 Verbena Drive

Heidi stepped onto the front porch to answer a phone call. She hated to interrupt her grandmother's story, but she decided she couldn't ignore the number any longer. "Hello?" she said as she sat down on the bottom step. "Yes…I know…I'm sorry, Josh." She started mindlessly pulling weeds from the flower bed while she listened to the frustrated voice on the other end. "I just need some time— Well, you'll just have to trust me." She stood up and brushed the bits of seeds and leaves from her lap. "I can't talk to you when you're like this. I'll call you later tonight…yes…I promise." She hung up, realizing too late that she didn't say *I love you, too.*

"Everything okay, honey?" Mo asked once she was back inside. She washed a plate and set it in the drainer rack by the sink.

"Yes…no…I don't know," Heidi answered. "That was Josh, my boyfriend."

"Is that right?" Mo smiled playfully.

"He asked me to marry him, and I just don't know what to say."

"Do you love him?"

"I thought I did, but if I really love him, why did I rent a car and drive across the country as soon as he asked me? Don't you think that's a bad sign?"

"Maybe." Mo was holding the Kentucky Derby spoon rest in her hand while she wiped it off with a dishtowel. "Why do *you* think you came here? I'm pleased as punch to see you, Doll Baby, but you haven't come to my house in years. Truth be known, I haven't heard from you since your Poppy's funeral. It sounds like you were leaving something behind as much as you were trying to get to something."

Heidi plopped back into the chair. Then she pressed her pointer fingers into the corners of her eyes and sighed. She felt like she could sleep for days, but she also wanted to climb up the wall or break something or go running down the street screaming.

"Tell me about this Josh fella," Mo said. She sat down opposite from Heidi and laid the spoon rest and dishtowel on the table.

"He's a screenwriter. We met at a party about six years ago, before either one of us had landed anything big. I was working at a day-care, and he was waiting tables. It was easier then…just a couple of kids with no money. Now I've got a project that's supposed to start shooting in a month and I'm the lead…the actual lead of a movie. It's called *Parabola*, and it's about a math teacher who has super powers and solves crimes. There's talk that it may become a franchise. It's my dream."

"And Josh doesn't want you to do it?" asked Mo.

"No, that's not it. He's all for it. He even helped me get an audition."

"So you feel like he's pushing you too much? Men can do that, you know. They say women are bossy, but it's my experience that men nearly always expect to be the boss."

Heidi smiled. "It's not that either. He's been really great. He has his own career, and he's been successful—everybody wants him to fix their scripts and take over when things are falling apart."

Mo counted off on her fingers as she said, "He isn't bossy, he helps you, he has a steady job…he must be ugly, like he hit every branch when he fell out of the ugly tree. Did I guess right? 'Cause looks aren't everything, honey. Unless he's an underwear model, his looks won't actually pay the bills."

Heidi chuckled as she pulled out her phone to show Mo a photo of Josh. "He definitely isn't ugly. See for yourself."

Mo adjusted her bifocals and squinted at the screen. "He looks alright to me. Just the right amount of muscles, if you know what I mean, and not too skinny. And I bet there's a real handsome face under that beard."

Heidi looked at the photo and thought about the day it was taken.

They had hiked up to Eagle Rock to see the views of the Santa Monica Mountains. It had been a gorgeous day, and the cliffs and canyons were breath-taking. Everything was perfect, but she had had that persistent feeling of pessimism which always gnawed at her when things were going well. It was like she heard her own voice whispering, *What goes up, must come down,* over and over again. She had battled that whisper since she was a little girl—balloons always pop, ice cream always melts, friendships never survive, good times never last. Normally, she could ignore it, act like everything was fine, because, after all, she was an actor. But this time she couldn't get past that feeling, and that's why she ran away.

"There's nothing wrong with Josh. It's me. There's something wrong with me." Heidi laid her forehead on the table and placed her hands on the back of her head. "It's like I have this secret desire to sabotage my own happiness."

Mo gently patted Heidi's arm. Then she picked up the Kentucky Derby spoon rest and carried it back to the stove, pausing for a moment as she traced the crack which went right down the center of the horse's face. It had been glued back together so many years ago, now the crevice was deeper where the glue had disintegrated. She set it down and turned to face Heidi.

"You know, they say there are two kinds of people in this world—ones who see the glass as half full and the other ones who see the glass as half empty, but I would say there are other types, too," said Mo. "There are those who get up and fill their own glasses and ones who fill up other people's for them. And then there are those who toss out the water in the glasses belonging to other people out of spite, and another group who toss out the water in their own glass, because they don't know just how thirsty they are and how hard it can be to come by good, clean water." She took the pitcher of iced tea from the refrigerator and refilled both of their glasses. "Now it sounds to me that you are the type who's afraid to even look at the glass."

With her face still mashed into the table, Heidi asked in a muffled voice, "What do I do? Should I marry him? What if Josh isn't The One? But if I turn him down, I may never find anyone else. Ugh! I'm so tired of feeling this way."

"That's probably part of the problem, honey. You're tired. Why don't you come back to the spare room and lay down for a bit? A nap can be the best thing for a weary traveler."

Heidi reluctantly agreed and followed Mo to the bedroom, past the bathroom and catty-corner to the master bedroom. Once she was in the little room, Heidi felt like she had stepped out of a time machine. The quilt made of teal and purple stars, the faux French provincial bureau and nightstand, the framed painting hanging above the headboard of a bonneted, little girl sitting on a fence overlooking a field of daisies—everything was just as she remembered it.

Mo pulled back the quilt and Heidi slid in. "Will you stay in here with me...just for a little while?" Heidi asked.

"I'd be happy to, Doll Baby."

Heidi scooted over and Mo lay down next to her.

"So what happened next?" asked Heidi, lying on her side. "Did the sheriff find out more about your mom?"

"Oh, Isham Brown was a nice man, but he wasn't one to keep hunting if the dogs stopped barking, if you know what I mean."

"No, not really." Heidi said as she stifled a yawn.

"He was a bit on the lazy side...and his son Ham wasn't much different, I tell ya...but it wasn't like Morgan's Hat was full of criminals, so he was a bit out of practice doing much police work. Sheriff Brown was all too happy to drop the case after a day of asking around. Some people just don't take enough pride in their work. But, of course, that wasn't the end of it for me."

illie drove to church the next morning and parked her Plymouth in its usual spot. Instead of entering the front door to head to the church offices, she walked over to the pastorium next door where Zeal had lived since the start of his employment with Berea Baptist. The church fathers—or at least their wives—had assumed the young, single pastor would get married and start a family soon after moving in, but this was not the case. Thirty-two years later and still unmarried, Zeal's life had remained mostly the same. Other than the addition of electricity and indoor plumbing, which were added in spite of Zeal's protests to the trustees and serving deacons that these were unnecessary extravagances, his residence hadn't changed much either.

It had been several years since Tillie had been inside the modest house with its metal roof and dark wood siding. As she was about to knock on the screen door, she thought about the last time she had visited the pastorium in late-1931. In bed with the flu, Zeal had missed services, a rare occurrence for Pastor Cooley. Tillie had stopped by on her way to the office the following Monday morning to bring Zeal a pot of chicken and dumplings and was horrified to find that his rooms were "not fit for a family of hogs." The next day, she had hired a woman from their church to clean and cook for him, and, as far as Tillie knew, the arrangement continued.

Flashbacks of seeing Zeal's filthy house which more resembled a remote hunting cabin scheduled for demolition than a respectable pastor's home produced feelings of self-reproach and compelled Tillie to make calculations of her culpability in the neglect of an innocent child. She had been so concerned with her quest to find the baby's mother, she hadn't considered if the pastor was up to the task or his home was fit for the care of a child. Tillie clutched the string of fat, purple beads she wore around her neck as she envisioned the possible calamities which might lie on the other side of the door. She heard no crying from within, but perhaps it was too quiet...even deathly quiet.

"Pastor! Pastor Cooley!" she yelled as she pounded on the wooden door frame. Tillie tried to peek in the window to the left of the door, but the curtains were drawn. "Hello! Anybody home?" She felt a swell of relief when Zeal finally opened the door with Moses resting against his shoulder.

"Mrs. Bransford," he whispered, "it sounds like you're leading Gideon's army to fight the Midianites right on my front porch! Why are you hollering?"

"I apologize," she whispered back as she tried to catch her breath and calm her heaving bosom. "I'm embarrassed to say that I assumed the worse when you didn't answer right away. I feared for little Moses...thought maybe something might've happened to her." She followed Zeal into the front room and felt further relief when she saw how clean the room was, even if it lacked any homey touches. Tillie felt that the placement of the crib in the center of the room was a bit inconvenient, but she thought this was not the best time to mention the tips about furniture placement which she had learned from her latest issue of *Good Housekeeping*.

"People do tend to act strange when it comes to little babies," Zeal said once he sat down in an armchair and shifted Moses to his other shoulder.

Tillie noticed that he looked tired, his eyes bloodshot and his chin covered in stubble. "Were you able to sleep?"

"Babies often get their days and nights mixed up, and this one seems to be suffering from that affliction." Zeal's voice was hoarse. "And she prefers to be held, which makes doing anything else mighty difficult."

"I'll make you some breakfast," Tillie said, hopping up. "Then I'll tell you all the news I learned last night."

In the kitchen, she made coffee and two fried eggs with buttered toast and brought it all in on a metal tray she had found underneath the sink. Zeal was snoring softly when she entered the front room. She set the tray on the side table and lifted the sleeping baby from his chest, gently laying her in the crib. Tillie watched Moses for a moment, marveling at the tiny infant's quivering lower lip as she decided if she would cry or continue napping. Moses soon found her fist and soothed herself. Tillie turned to see that Zeal was awake and studying her.

"Thank you for the food, Mrs. Bransford," he said as he reached for the tray. "I sure am hungry."

"I would've let you sleep if I'd-a known you were so tired."

"I'm not one to sleep when the sun is up, anyhow." He took a swig of the hot coffee. "I never would've thought to use this tray for serving food. I always do admire your resourcefulness."

Tillie regarded the odd-looking tray which resembled the curved blade of a shovel with a U-shaped portion removed from the flat side. "Oh? What is it?" she asked.

"This is a neck tray from my uncle's funeral parlor. It rests real nicely on the deceased's chest while you're working on the body." Zeal leaned back and demonstrated the positioning of the tray on himself. "Before I went to seminary, I lived in Arkansas for a portion of time and worked in a funeral parlor. Uncle Uriah never quite forgave me for leaving the mortuary business. He wanted me to take it over, but I soon realized it wasn't for me. All he left me when he died was a few rusty pieces like this."

"Lands sake! I downright forgot you were ever in that line of work," Tillie responded weakly. She felt a little light-headed at the thought of dead bodies being in close proximity to the tray on which the pastor was now eating his eggs and toast. She did draw some comfort from the knowledge that she had thoroughly disinfected the dusty tray before using it.

"Oh, yes. I did all manner of tasks for Uncle Uriah at his place, including but not limited to hair and makeup. Not to sound boastful, but I developed quite a knack at making flower arrangements, too. You'd think that handling the bodies would be the most awful part of the job, but the part I disliked the most was taking photographs of the deceased. It was common for poorer families to have no photographs of their loved ones in their living bodies, so they looked at that moment before the casket was closed and covered with dirt as their last chance. Furthermore, they'd often say that Pa or Sister never looked better, so why not get their picture on celluloid. It just made me feel so sorrowful, like Jesus weeping at the death of his friend Lazarus."

Tillie listened carefully to Zeal's recollection of his duties at the funeral home. She noticed that his coffee cup was empty, so she hopped up to get the pot from the kitchen to refill it.

"You said you had news about Moses' mother," Zeal said as he sopped up the runny yolk with his toast. "What did you discover?"

"Well, I asked myself who would most likely possess information from twenty or so years ago." Tillie returned to her seat, delighted to recount the details of her mission and leave behind the discussion of the mortuary industry. "I called on a few of our older townspeople, the ones with all their faculties who might like a little company. I was like a bee, flitting from flower to flower! One bit of gossip would take me to the next, and so on. I finally landed on Mrs. Putnam, great matriarch of the Putnam family and keeper of all that happens on the south side of town. And here's what I learned: Do you remember Willadeene Lathrop who lived in that big house up on Harley Hill? She was rich as a Rockefeller—well, at least in Morgan's Hat money—anyhow, Mrs. Putnam told me that Miss Willadeene had a great niece who would come and stay with her from time to time, just a week in the summer but pretty regular. She can't recall the niece's name, but she did say Miss Willadeene loved to tell how this girl was real accomplished musically. She even paid to send her to some fancy music school up North. Mrs. Putnam said the girl wasn't able to make it to Morgan's Hat for Miss Willadeene's funeral back in '34, because she was in school and couldn't get a train that would have her here in time for services. Mrs. Putnam thought it was scandalous for the girl to miss the funeral of her only living—well, recently living—relative, but I would venture to guess that Marjorie Putnam has rarely traveled outside of Davis County and doesn't realize how difficult train travel can be, especially back then." Tillie paused to take a breath. "So I'm going to head over to the old Lathrop house and see if the current residents know anything about the niece. They are Episcopalians from Shreveport, but I hear they're good people."

Moses began to stir in the crib. She drew in her legs, balled her tiny fists, scrunched up her face, and then heartily filled her diaper.

Zeal smiled through his sigh. "I believe it will be less problematic for me to work on my sermon from home today," he said. "I'll get done what I can and rely on you to report back what you hear."

Before the diaper pins were unfastened, Tillie was out the screen door and on her way to the big house on Harley Hill.

374 Verbena Drive

When Heidi woke up, she felt disoriented. It was that dusky hour when the sun is mostly gone, but before the sky was dark enough to see the stars. With the change in the colors of the room, it felt like she had slept not for hours, but for days, or even whole seasons had come and gone. "Mo?" Heidi called, but she was alone in the room. She threw off the quilt and sat up, stretching her back and massaging her achy shoulders.

Heidi walked into the kitchen and called for her grandmother again, but all she saw was a simmering pot of chicken and dumplings, the sides of the stockpot streaked with burnt strips where the pot had boiled over. The thick, bubbling soup was topped off with a thin film made from the congealed fats of the chicken broth. She turned off the stove and continued her search.

She stepped onto the Astroturf floor of the screened-in back porch, pausing just long enough to breathe in the musty smell of the cushions tied to the metal rockers, before going out to the backyard where she finally found Mo standing under the weeping willow tree. She was wearing a short gardening apron full of small tools. As she tugged branches loose and placed them in a large, plastic container by her feet, Mo sang softly in a shaky, vibrato voice. Heidi could just makes out the words to her song:

Chippy, chip, chip. The sparrow sings a song.
He wonders if you like his hat and if you'll sing along.
He whistles to his lady bird to say his love is strong.

He tells her that forever feels just like a day is long.
Yes, forever with his darling sparrow flies by like birdsong.

"Mo—what are you doing out here?" Heidi asked.

"Oh, I'm just working on my special project." Mo continued combing through the low branches without turning around. "You have a good nap?"

"Yes ma'am. I feel a lot better."

"I've got supper on the stove, if you're hungry."

"Yeah, it smells great. I'll get some in a minute." Heidi listened to her grandmother's humming, and then she asked, "What kind of project are you working on? What do you do with all these branches?"

Mo smiled and said, "Grab that bin and come with me."

Heidi obeyed, following her to a shed in the corner of the yard. Once there, Mo threw open the double doors and flipped the switch on a hanging lightbulb. "Ta-da! My special project!"

As the bulb swung a shaft of light back and forth inside the dark space, Heidi saw what was filling nearly every inch of the 8x10-foot shed—a variety of empty, woven birdhouses. There were tall skinny ones, and fat short ones, and everything in between. Heidi noticed some had large gaps between the slats, while others were woven in a close, dense design with a round hole near the bottom. It seemed that Mo never repeated the same pattern, so each one was different.

"These are amazing," Heidi said. "But what are you making them for?"

"It started back when your Poppy was sick. He liked for me to set up a folding chair for him to sit under the weeping willow. He would sit there for hours. I think he mostly liked being outside and the tree gave him some shade, but he also liked telling me what to do, like I was his feet and hands since he couldn't get around too good. 'Sugar, you missed some weeds over there,' he'd say. Anyhow, I stayed pretty busy caring for him—keeping him comfortable, helping him bathe, making sure he got his medicines—but it finally got to be too much for me, and I had to take him to an old folks' home. It hurt me, at first, felt like I was shirking my duty as his wife. But I could see that it was best for him, and I would visit every day. I still had hope that he would get better—which was foolish—but the hope kept both our spirits up. After a while, the doctors said Jimbo had a few weeks left, and then he was gone." Mo picked up a smaller birdhouse and set it in the corner on top of a several larger ones.

"The day he died, I came home and stood under that tree and yelled at the Lord. I asked God why He always takes things away from me, and why did I have to be all alone. Before I knew it, I was ripping down every willow branch I could get my hands on. It didn't matter that my fingers were bleeding, and I was scratching up my face and arms I was so mad that night." Mo began sorting the branches into two groups by bending them, testing their flexibility. In one pile she put the straight ones which were thicker and in the other pile she placed the curved, thinner branches.

"So making these birdhouses helped you while you were grieving?" Heidi asked, prompting Mo to continue her story.

"Well, that came a little later." Mo turned around to look at the tree, but Heidi couldn't stop looking at her grandmother. The old woman seemed to be watching the willow tree as if it were an old friend she expected any minute to turn, look back at her, and wave. "You see, I hated that tree," Mo went on. "A weeping willow is a messy, weak thing, meant to grow by river banks, not in the middle of a backyard. Your Poppy planted it there years ago, and I couldn't stand the sight of it. But he always told me that it would grow on me. Well, that night that I lost him, when I yelled and shook my fist at God and tore up the branches, I eventually wore myself out. My tantrum soon petered out, and I dropped to my knees and cried. I was just a lump on the ground, ready to melt into the dirt and stay there forever, when a breeze swooped in. It lifted those willowy branches and swung them around until they were hugging me, wrapping their arms around me, giving me comfort." Mo was still staring at the tree as she caressed one of the thin branches in her hand. "I know I sound like a foolish, old woman—and that's probably because I am one—but it was a moment I hope I never forget."

Heidi pulled her attention away from Mo and looked at the willow tree with its backdrop of grayish-purple streaks peeking through the spaces between the long branches. Closest to the tree trunk, where the shadows were thickest, Heidi tried to imagine her grandmother's crumpled form, grief-stricken and angry.

Heidi's imaginings were interrupted by Mo's loud snuffle. "It's getting too dark to do much more tonight," she said as she switched off the light and shut the shed doors. "You need to eat some supper, anyhow."

"But what are all those birdhouses for?" Heidi asked as they walked back toward the lights shining through the kitchen windows. "Do you sell them? I bet you could make a ton of money at a farmer's market or a craft fair. I could even get you set up with an account online."

"Nah, honey, I don't mess with selling them. It just wouldn't feel right. You see, I used to fuss every time I had to go around picking up those branches from the yard. I thought it was such a chore! Then the tree hugged me and…well, I can't tell you the next part 'cause you'll think I'm crazy—"

Heidi grabbed her grandmother's wrinkled hand. "No! I won't think you're crazy. Please tell me."

"Alright, if you promise not to lock me up in the looney bin…the night your Poppy died, the tree hugged me and whispered something to me. It said…" Mo cleared her throat to prepare her delivery of the tree's message, then, in a spooky voice, she said, "*And lo! The fowls of the heaven have their habitation and sing among the branches.*" Mo paused for effect. When Heidi didn't respond, she explained, "The willow always talks like a King James' Bible."

"Oh, well— Did it say anything else?"

"Yes, the next day I came back out and stood under the tree again before I had to go make arrangements at the funeral home. I wanted to hear another word, something encouraging to help me make sense of all the pain I was troubled by. This time the tree said, *A mustard seed was cast into a garden. It grew into a great tree, and the fowls of the air lodged in its branches.*"

They were standing inside the dark back porch now and still holding hands. "So you felt like the tree was telling you to make birdhouses?" Heidi asked, trying to keep even a speck of sarcasm or doubt from her voice.

"I s'pose so. It felt like my mustard seed was to take something I didn't want—those branches from the tree I hated—and make them into something for the birds who were living out there. I needed to be grateful, even for the hard times." Mo patted Heidi's hand before releasing it. "The world can be a rough place, Doll Baby. We need to help out the little fellas as much as we can, and sometimes that starts with us doing something small, taking a tiny step in the direction of being useful."

Morgan's Hat, Tennessee, 1941

Tillie stood beside her Plymouth and stared up at the giant Victorian house perched at the top of Harley Hill. Though the siding was a muted shade of pink and the trim work around the windows, doors, and gables was a complementary mauve, there was something inherently intimidating about the design of the house. Of course, the steep pitch of the rooflines and the asymmetrical towers and turrets jutting up in intervals with the various chimneys played a role in the home's unapproachable façade.

Grasping a plate of cookies she had hastily thrown together and covered with a dishtowel, Tillie climbed the stairs to the spacious wrap-around porch. She rang the doorbell and listened to the elegant eight-note chimes from within.

A petite, older woman answered the door. Tillie quickly assessed the woman's appearance. She was wearing an understated, black dress and a string of pearls. Her black hair was lined with distinguished streaks of gray and gathered at the nape of her neck in a slightly dated, if not somehow aloof, bun. "Yes?" the woman intoned in a rich voice which reminded Tillie of an impenetrable swamp. "May I help you?"

"My name is Chantilly Bransford, and I'm the church secretary at Berea Baptist. I so wanted to come by and meet you, seeing that you're new to Morgan's Hat." Tillie offered to hand her the plate of cookies, but the woman's arms remained motionless at her sides, mimicking the lack of change in her facial expression. "I'd love to visit with you for a spell," Tillie continued, undaunted, "and fill you in on the doings of our fair town."

The woman sighed then replied, "We are hardly new to town. We have lived on this hill for more than six months. And I feel I should tell you that Mr. Gautreaux and I are dedicated Episcopalians." She mentioned her religious affiliation while narrowing her eyes at the covered plate in Tillie's hands, as if it held some strange, indigestible Baptist delicacy. "But please, do come in."

The woman led the way to a formal parlor with soaring ceilings, stiff-backed furniture, and tasseled draperies shrouding the tall windows. Tillie sat on a firm, velvet settee and placed the cookies on the table in front of her. Once the woman was seated in an armchair across from her, Tillie said, "I don't believe I caught your first name, Mrs. Gautreaux…"

"Ophelia," the woman responded, her hands folded demurely in her lap. "Mr. Gautreaux and I moved here from Shreveport after he sold his shares in the family business."

"Oh? And what business was that?"

"Oil," was all Ophelia said in response.

"I see. And what brought you to Morgan's Hat?" asked Tillie.

"My husband's cousin lives in Palmyra, and she told him about this house when it became vacant. Since boyhood, Mr. Gautreaux has been prone to fevers, so he wanted to move away from Louisiana's damp climate. Moreover, he has always wanted to live on a high hill, so he was obliged to move us…*here*." Her last word was spoken with exposed disdain. Tillie could tell that the move had not been Ophelia Gautreaux's idea.

"So you didn't know the woman who lived here before you—Miss Willadeene Lathrop?" Ophelia shook her head almost imperceptibly. "Oh…well, I believe Miss Willadeene was born right in this very house," Tillie continued. "Her daddy, Asa Lathrop, built the house for his new wife. Many called it the Lathrop Mansion. Miss Willadeene never married, though I'm sure she had many offers. She always seemed to think of herself as a pretty, young girl. Every time I saw her in person or in photographs, she had a wreath of flowers in her hair, like she was heading to a debutante ball or some other grand party.

In the years that I knew her, especially near the end, she was a bit of a recluse, though she would come to services at the church when she was feeling up to it. I don't know that she had any surviving relatives."

"I am not aware of any," Ophelia replied. "But we know very little about Miss Lathrop."

"I wonder if you found anything left behind when you moved in. Perhaps something of the family's that wasn't sold when the whole lot went up for auction?" asked Tillie, hopefully. "Maybe some papers or photographs?"

"All that was in this house when Mr. Gautreaux bought it was an unholy amount of dirt, dust, and a family of filthy rodents."

They both sat in silence for an awkward moment. Tillie sensed that this woman was clearly eager for her to leave, but Ophelia's well-bred manners were all that was preventing her from revealing just how much she wanted this unexpected visitor gone. Even knowing this about her hostess, Tillie wasn't ready to give up on her search yet. She eventually interrupted the silence by asking, "Do you have any children, Mrs. Gautreaux?"

Ophelia's shoulders slumped forward, and she nodded. "I have a daughter. Her name is Lorraine." She picked up a small, silver picture frame on the end table and showed it to Tillie. "She's married to a…a…farmer." Ophelia dissolved into tears. Between sobs she blurted out, "Lives in Jackson…grows sugar cane…she wears men's trousers…years of finishing school wasted!"

"There, there, Mrs. Gautreaux. It can't be as bad as all that." Tillie reached to pat Ophelia's knee, but the inconsolable mother pulled away. "Farming is an honest, decent living," Tillie went on. "I'm sure your daughter's situation has some real favorable points."

"Aw, mais, la!" yelled Ophelia, betraying her Cajun roots the more upset she became. "That peeshwank girl o' mine! And there's nothing I can do about it up here in this moche house! When Lorraine married my couillon son-in-law, I knew she'd be poor and poor she is, that fuh sure!" Ophelia took a deep breath and set the picture frame back on the end table. She smoothed the folds of her dress and returned her hands to her lap. "Please forgive me, Mrs. Bransford. I don't rightly know what came over me."

"If you don't mind me saying, I think you need to get out more. Make friends. Go shopping downtown. Plant roses. Join the church choir," said Tillie. "Your daughter may have chosen a life you didn't want her to have, but *you* can still be happy."

Tillie remained at the house, visiting with Ophelia and listening to her talk about her daughter for more than an hour. She was shown a family photo album and given a tour of the house, or at least the rooms on the first floor. Ophelia tried to convince her to stay for a light lunch, but Tillie explained that she needed to get back to the church and type up the pastor's sermon notes.

"I am so glad you came by this morning," Ophelia said as she stood with Tillie at the door. "I will take your advice and invite Lorraine and Oliver up for the holidays."

"Good! You'll be glad you did."

"And thank you for those delicious tea cakes you brought," said Ophelia.

Tillie was holding an empty plate in one hand and a folded dish-towel in the other. "I'll be sure to get you the recipe. It came from my sweet neighbor, Miss Eloise. They're easy as anything to make. The key to the recipe is one cup of good, fresh buttermilk."

"Recipe...oh, that reminds me. Please, wait a moment, won't you?" Ophelia left and returned a few minutes later with a little wooden box with a hinged lid. "You asked about anything we might've found in the house—this was in the kitchen behind the pie safe." She opened the box, revealing a jumbled stack of recipe cards. "If you find any distant Lathrop relatives, perhaps you can give this to them."

"I sure will!" Tillie smiled gratefully as she took the box. "There's a good chance I've already found one."

374 Verbena Drive

After she had eaten a soupy bowl of Mo's chicken and dumplings, Heidi went out to her rental car to retrieve her overnight bag. Her grandmother wouldn't allow her to help clean the kitchen, so she decided a hot shower would be the best thing to release the tightening in her shoulders and neck and hopefully get her in a more agreeable mood to call Josh back.

Once she was in her favorite cotton pajamas, she lay on her stomach on the purple and teal quilt in the spare bedroom to make the call. "Hey, Josh," she said. She noticed that he answered after the first ring. Heidi had to give it to him—Josh didn't play games, an unusual and refreshing quality in a film industry boyfriend.

They talked around the subject of her hasty disappearance without really discussing it, until he finally asked her why she had left. "Was it me? Was it something I did?" he asked.

"It's 100% me—seriously. I think everything was moving so fast with the production schedule and you asking...you know..." Somehow she couldn't finish the sentence.

"Asking you to marry me? Geez, Heidi, you can't even say the words, so I'm guessing you can't say *yes*, either."

"Please don't give up on me. I'm working through some stuff; stuff from growing up without really knowing anything about my family. I'll give you an example: I lived with my grandparents for the whole year I was in kindergarten. My parents had split up, and neither one of them was in a place where they could take care of me. I didn't see my grandparents much after that, but a whole year of my life was spent with these two people I called Mo and Poppy. I found out today that, as a baby, Mo was left on a doorstep of a church to be raised by a middle-aged pastor. An actual doorstep! It's like a 1940s version of *Silas Marner*."

"That's a really intriguing plotline, but what does it have to do with you?" asked Josh.

"Don't you see? This is part of my story, too, and I don't know anything about it...or I didn't until a few hours ago. I need to sit with my grandmother and talk through some of this family history. I can't talk to my mom about it. She would rather pretend that nothing bad ever happens to anybody...anywhere...anytime. Mo's the only person alive who can give me this. And being here helps me remember things, memories that show me what I need to ask her. I'm realizing that I've been living without any answers partly because I don't even know the questions to ask."

"So, can you at least tell me you're not saying *no* to me, to us?"

"I'm not saying *no*," Heidi replied firmly. "I know I need to get back to L.A., and I will." She waited a beat before continuing, listening to Josh's breathing for hints of his disappointment in her or even a sudden, clarifying recognition that he was having second thoughts about their future together. She mostly just heard the tiny whistle his nose made when he was concentrating really hard, and his deviated septum couldn't adjust to the increased air flow.

"Do you want me to come to Tennessee?" he asked. "I've got a few meetings the next couple of days, but I can reschedule them."

"No, but I really appreciate you offering. I really do...I'll call you tomorrow...I love you."

"Love you, too."

After they hung up, Heidi felt better knowing that she actually remembered to say *I love you*, and she had said it first this time. She also realized with surprise that she missed that little nose whistle. Maybe he was *The One* after all.

Morgan's Hat, Tennessee, 1941

When Tillie returned to the church, she walked back to the pastorium to show Pastor Cooley the recipe box. She hadn't taken the time to look through the cards inside yet. It felt like cheating to start examining them before she could share her find, and Tillie was just superstitious enough to feel like she'd be jinxing her mission if she made any selfish, overconfident missteps.

After she had knocked on the door, Zeal called for her to come in, and she found him feeding Moses a bottle. "Pastor, I think I may have found a clue," she exclaimed, attempting to conceal her enthusiasm in case the recipe box turned out to be a dead end. "This is a box of recipe cards belonging to the late Miss Willadeene Lathrop."

"So you found something from the family?" said Zeal. "That is surprising since the house stood empty for more than five years after Miss Willadeene's passing. I thought the bank had sold off all the household goods—lock, stock, and barrel."

"Well, Mrs. Gautreaux—who, by the way, is much nicer than what you might hear in town—she praised my baking and asked for my tea cake recipe. Anyhow, she found this box behind a cupboard. I'm just thrilled she hadn't thrown it away. It was Divine Providence that made her hold on to it, I'd wager. She doesn't come across as a gushy, sentimental-type person." Tillie watched Zeal gently wipe Moses' milky mouth with a burp cloth, then continued. "As soon as I'm finished typing up your sermon, I'll get started looking through these recipe cards. Hopefully, they'll lead me to family names that might help me find the poor little one's mama."

"Well, I haven't exactly had a chance to write out my sermon yet, what with taking care of Moses. Maybe I'll just read the whole book of Haggai this Sunday. It's only two chapters and all about rebuilding the Temple. Maybe the board of deacons will glean from the text a renewed sense of urgency to finish the Sunday school classrooms which we drew up plans for back in '38."

"I don't know that they will automatically make that connection, Pastor. Haggai may be a short book, but from the congregation's response to your reading Habakkuk each week for the entire month of July, I can't say how effective it will be." Tillie rarely ever commented on Zeal's sermons, but she woke up feeling particularly energized that morning. Maybe it was the crispness in the Fall air or the stimulating mission to help reunite a mother and child. Or maybe it was the fact that she had just finished reading *The Murder at the Vicarage* and imagined herself a clever female detective the likes of Miss Marple, and she wanted to get busy investigating. "I will hunt through my files of your old sermons. Then I'll type up something for you to look at and bring it over this afternoon. Would that suit you?"

"Thank you, Mrs. Bransford. I feel as though I'm leaving too much for you to do, but I see that you are more than capable."

Tillie looked at the rumpled little man holding the tiny baby and felt a strange warmth for the scene. Was it a yearning? Some kind of long-suppressed desire? Before responding, she smoothed the waves of her pompadour and felt the scar along the edge of her hairline. The warmth faded, and Tillie's devotion to her mission was renewed.

At the church office, Tillie pulled out a file from one of the drawers in the tall, metal filing cabinet and set the sheaf of papers on her desk. She threaded a piece of blank paper onto the platen rollers of her typewriter and began by typing Zeal's customary introduction to Sunday services:

```
Good morning and welcome to the Lord's
  House at Berea Baptist church.
```

Then she paused as her hands hovered over the keys. She glanced at the old sermon lying next to the typewriter. She read the cold, hard words and the rambling exegesis of the text. Tillie lifted her hands and lowered them again a few times, but her fingers just refused to type anything else.

Instead, she opened one of her desk drawers and pulled out a black leather-bound Bible. She found the Gospels, read a page and a half, then turned back to her typewriter. She resumed typing, her fingers flying to keep up with her thoughts. In less than an hour, she had six, full pages filled, in addition to the note cards Zeal like to hold as he preached. As was her routine for the last twenty years, she stacked the sheets and the notes together, adding a small paper clip to the upper left corner.

With the sermon completed, Tillie began taking cards out of the recipe box. She spread them out across her desk, reading the smudged titles of the dishes and the smeared names of the recipes' authors. There were greasy splotches and dried bits of batter speckled haphazardly over most them.

Spicy Peach Chutney...Myra Parker
Leona Dansby's Catfish Croquettes
Prune Pudding from Norma Peters
Mabel Jenkins' Banana Cake

Tillie recognized the names on the cards, most of them now deceased, but women whose families still lived in the area. "Lola Tharpe's got several desserts here: Coconut Cake, Lemon Cheese Cake, and Lady Baltimore Cake. Oh my...here's Mrs. Malcom Mosely's recipe for Corned Beef Luncheon Salad—lemon gelatin, beef broth, lemon juice, can of corned beef, three hard-boiled eggs, celery, onion, and mayonnaise. Heaven help the saints at the potluck!"

She continued through the stack, making notes of names and copying recipes which piqued her interest, until she got to the last two. "Jam Layer Cake from Royal L. Whitman and Hawaiian Wedding Cake from Tabitha Langford. All done."

She created her own identification system for the names. By the ones which she recognized as townspeople of Morgan's Hat, she wrote *MH* for the town's name. For the names which Tillie recognized as frequent visitors to Morgan's Hat, such as Myra Parker,

Sheriff Brown's mother-in-law, she wrote a *V* for visitor. There were five names which she couldn't identify at all. Tillie circled these names in her notes and added a question mark next to each of them. Could one of these women be a relative of Baby Moses? At least it was a place to start.

"Five o'clock already," said Tillie after she had looked at her wrist-watch. "I'd better get this sermon over to the Pastor."

Tillie tore the sheet from her legal pad where she had listed the women's names and folded it before slipping it inside her purple handbag. She hustled over to the pastorium to drop off the sermon.

"Pastor," Tillie began. She had just left the typed packet on the end table and was turning to leave. "I made a few changes to your message for Sunday…"

Moses was attempting to squirm away from Zeal as he changed her diaper on the sofa. Through the safety pins clenched between his gritted teeth, he replied, "Oh, I'm sure it's fine, Mrs. Bransford. I'll take a look at it tomorrow."

"Yessir." She hesitated at the door, unsure if she'd done enough to help. "I know tomorrow's Saturday, but feel free to ring me if you need anything. You could just use the phone at the office and ask the switchboard…"

"I appreciate that," Zeal interjected, "but I think I'll be fine. My sister Seraphim is coming in from Mt. Pleasant to spend the weekend with us. News sure does travel fast! When she heard I was looking after a baby, she sent word through Silas Padgett that she would be here sometime Saturday morning. My nephew is driving her up." Freshly changed, Moses was lying on her back and cooing happily as her arms and legs flailed haphazardly. "I hope I'm not one to be too proud to admit when I need assistance from others, but I feel a little disappointed that Sera is coming, though she will be of great help during services. I can't rightly hold Moses and preach at the same time!"

"No, I don't suppose you can," Tillie replied. As she walked to her Plymouth, she couldn't help but wonder what Zeal would say when he read his sermon and its unmistakable lack of Haggai or Habakkuk.

374 Verbena Drive

Heidi walked through the kitchen and down the three steps into the den which had once been a two-car garage. Sitting in a country blue recliner and her eyes focused on a movie she was watching on the television, Mo peeled the thin bark from the willow branches which were soaking in the bin at her feet.

Heidi was combing her wet hair as she entered. "What are you watching?" she asked.

"Aw, some scary movie about bank robbers. I was watching *Wheel of Fortune*, then this movie started. I couldn't find the remote to change it, so I just left it on. Now I'm so wrapped up in finding out if that bald fella there is gonna pull off the robbery, that I can't seem to stop watching it. One good thing about watching this kind of movie on TV is that they have to take out all the swear words." Mo pointed to the screen with a branch she held in her wet hand. "See that fella right there? The one with all the tattoos on his face? Before you came in here, he looked at that other fella on his team, the one with the mouth full of metal fillings and the bolt through his eyebrow, and said in a real nasty voice, *Joke you.* I may be an old lady who listens to talking trees, but I'm pretty sure he actually said a real cuss word. There's quite a bit of shooting, and most of the women have on as much clothes as a boiled chicken, but at least they cleaned up the language."

Mo noticed Heidi was struggling with the comb. "Put a couple of pillows on the floor here," Mo said, "And I'll comb your hair for you."

"Really?" asked Heidi.

"I would love to! I could even give you a braid or two, just like I did when you lived with us."

Heidi obeyed and took three pillows from the sofa and threw them onto the floor in front of Mo. She handed her the comb and sat down.

"I don't recall your hair being this shade, and it sure has gotten long," said Mo as she gently worked on a tangle.

"The studio wanted me to go really light blonde for this role, and they asked me to grow it out. I've never liked having long hair. It's too much work to keep it from looking like a blonde rat's nest. I'm so ready to chop it all off."

"Oh! Don't do that! It's so pretty! It just needs a little T.L.C. Let me run and get something. I'll be right back." Mo hopped up and returned a few minutes later with a plastic spray bottle. Heidi saw that it was full of a creamy green-colored liquid.

"What is that?" Heidi asked, dubiously.

"Just a little conditioner and hot water," Mo replied. "It'll get those knots untangled in a jiffy."

As soon as she began spraying the warm mixture, Heidi was transported to that very place—sitting at her grandmother's feet as she combed out her long hair. "Green apples," Heidi murmured.

"What was that, honey?"

"It smells like green apples." Heidi felt like she was five years old again, missing her parents and engulfed in worry. In her mind, she was clinging to her grandmother like a lifeboat stuck in the middle of an ocean full of gale-force winds. She thought, *It's strange how a smell can remind me of something I haven't thought of in decades.*

Once her hair was smooth, Mo divided it into two parts to start braiding. Her nimble fingers, the same ones which made those intricately-woven bird houses, easily plaited the wet hair. "All done," said Mo as she handed Heidi the comb.

"Thank you," Heidi said as she stood up and carried the pillows back to the sofa.

"It was my pleasure, honey," Mo replied.

Heidi sat on the sofa, stretching out her legs, then digging her bare feet under the cushion.

"Grab that afghan from the back of the couch if your feet are cold, honey," Mo instructed.

As Heidi pulled the crocheted blanket across her and removed her feet from their burrowing position, she noticed a long strip of silver duct tape on the edge of the sofa cushion. The peeling tape reminded her of the time her grandfather had helped her build a blanket fort in the den. To keep the blankets in place, Poppy had given her long strips of duct tape. Then he had given her a flashlight covered with a piece of red cellophane to set on the floor and pretend it was a campfire. She had asked to sleep there all night, and her grandparents had agreed. Heidi remembered that when it was time for bed, Mo had slept in the recliner all night so that she wouldn't be scared.

Heidi now stared at the television without really watching the movie, trying to rein in her unanticipated emotions connected to these long-dormant memories. In the middle of a scene, it cut to a commercial, and she was snapped back to her present reality. She cleared her throat and swallowed past the threatening tears. "What happened to my mom and dad? Were you surprised that they didn't stay together?"

"I don't blame your Mama. Phillip had a lot of problems. Sure, they were happy at first, but when he hurt his back at work, then he started in with the pills, well, it got bad. They were so young when they had you…but that's just making excuses." Mo picked up a thin willow branch and bent it into a circle. "I never stopped loving him and hoping he would get better. That's what a mother does. Then when he got sent up…" The movie had begun again, and Mo looked at the television. "Well, it all fell apart after that."

"I shouldn't have asked," Heidi said in a small voice. "I just feel like I don't know anything about the time before I came here to live with you and Poppy. Don't you think it's weird that I don't remember very much about us all—me and Mom and Dad—living together? It's like my life started when Mom brought me here. Then I remember the summer after kindergarten, when she came and got me and brought me to Atlanta. What am I missing?"

"It hurts to have a chunk of your story gone. It's like that feeling when you're leaving the Piggly Wiggly and you know you forgot to buy something, but you can't remember what."

"Except this isn't just forgetting to buy milk at the grocery store," Heidi's voice grew louder and sharper. "This is my life!"

Mo wiped her hands on a faded pink hand towel she had spread across her lap. "It used to be that people would sit on front porches and visit. You would walk around town and get the news about their kin. People would tell old stories, stories that were handed down from generation to generation. Those stories are how come I know what I know about the time when *I* was a baby. They're like family jewels, so precious, and you deserve to know about your daddy. It's only fair."

Heidi felt guilty that she had raised her voice to her grandmother. She noticed how tired she looked and thought for the first time since she had arrived, how lonely she must be. "It's getting late. And I don't want to keep you up," said Heidi.

"I can't sleep more than four hours a night anymore. I usually get a few cat naps in during the day, so that helps. It's just part of being an old fogey, I s'pose."

"Well, I'm not really sleepy either."

"How about this? I'll go pop us some popcorn, and we'll have a good talk." Mo stood up and dug her hand in the sides of the seat of her recliner, lifting up the cushion. "And you see if you can find that dadgum remote and turn off the TV."

"Are you sure?" Heidi regretted bringing up the subject. It felt selfish and cruel.

Mo cupped Heidi's chin in her hand. "I'd do anything for you, Doll Baby, 'cuz I love you from here to the hereafter and ten miles past that."

Morgan's Hat, Tennessee, 1941

Seraphim, Zeal's older sister, was dropped off at his house at 10:00 a.m. Saturday morning. Before suppertime, she had assembled three casseroles—one made primarily of chicken and rice to eat that evening and two others to freeze for later—made from the groceries she had picked up from the Piggly Wiggly just south of Morgan's Hat. The stop took her—and her grown son Leonard who was driving her—on a roundabout route from her home in Mt. Pleasant, but Seraphim had wanted to quickly stop by to check in on an elderly cousin who lived in Hurricane Mills.

"Zeal," Seraphim shouted from the kitchen, "I'm putting a crock of Brunswick Stew and a pan of smothered chops to freeze in your Frigidaire. I'll write out how you should cook them."

Zeal entered the kitchen carrying Moses so that she was chest down along his forearm with her cheek resting in his palm. The baby girl was fully awake and smiling. "Thank you, Sister. That is mighty kind."

Seraphim looked at Zeal and exclaimed, "Heavens! Why are you holding that child in such a peculiar way? She's not a football! They say that if a baby is held with its brain pitched down too often it can't do 'rithmetic in its head when it gets older."

"She likes it," answered Zeal, a little defensively. "Truth is, she'd ruther be held this way than any other. You know every baby has its preference when it comes to things like this. I remember Leonard liked it if I held him upside-down by his big toes when he was little. He would squeal and laugh till he was fit to split."

"Pshaw." Seraphim rolled her eyes. "Well, Leonard weren't a new-born baby when you did that. If I recall correctly, he was asking for you to do it, so he must've at least been old enough to talk."

"I reckon you're right." Zeal reevaluated the slope of his arm and made a slight correction.

Seraphim untied her apron, folded it neatly, and placed it in the basket she had brought from home. "I've been working in the kitchen since I got here, and we haven't had a chance to chitchat. Let's sit a while so I can put my feet up."

Zeal followed her into the living room and laid Moses in the fruit crate which was sitting on the floor and still lined with the pale pink blanket. Seraphim had suggested he put the crib in the spare bedroom instead of leaving it in the middle of the living room. She had also found space in the closet of the spare bedroom for a metal green baby walker and a wooden high chair decorated with a decoupaged picture of a lamb, along with the clothes which were too large for the baby, to keep them out of the way until Moses was old enough to use them.

He plopped himself down on the sofa, and Seraphim settled herself in the armchair, resting her feet on a little stool. She crossed her arms under breasts and asked, "Now as to this baby business—how long do you expect to keep this up?" She pursed her lips disapprovingly. Seraphim was eight years older than Zeal and taller by several inches. He flinched at the withering skepticism in her voice and felt as if he were being scolded, like the time when he was four years old and attempted to chop wood behind the house like the older children. Seraphim had snatched the axe from his hands and said, "You don't know what you're doing! Give me that before somebody gets hurt!"

"I showed you the letter, Sera. I'm obliged to..." he began.

"You're obliged to do what's right and proper for this baby. She needs a real family, and though it would be uncharitable to say that you've been careless with the child in the ways you've tended to her..." She paused, assessing her partial compliment. Zeal thought Seraphim seemed disappointed to admit he'd actually done a good job without her constant guidance. "You have to agree that you can't be her father. You're an old bachelor."

"I am old and a bachelor, but I'm also willing to do what I must for Moses." Zeal looked at the baby in the crate and felt a smile stretch across his face. Against his better judgement and his best attempts at regarding Moses as if she were any other poor, vulnerable creature in need, he was getting attached. "You should know that Mrs. Bransford, my secretary, is out looking for Moses' kin. We don't want to send her off to some children's home in Nashville or Memphis, but I promise to do right by her, one way or th'other."

"Chantilly Bransford…she still unmarried?" Seraphim asked.

Zeal was relieved by the change in subject—his sister rarely gave up on an argument she hadn't won outright—but he was wary of where she was going with this new line of questions. "Yes," he answered.

"Her husband's been gone a long time. I'm surprised she's not found a new one. Any men come to court her?"

"Well, how should I know that?" Zeal replied much louder than he meant to. He regained his self-possession, silently reciting the nine Fruits of the Spirit as was his habit when he felt overcome, then continued, "I am not one to partake of idle gossip, Sister. You should know that it's the devil's hobby to stir up that kind of talk in a small town like ours."

"It's not gossiping to be interested in the lives and good fortune of others. My, you're touchy! I was just asking because if you carry on with this idea of adopting Moses, you could provide a better home for her if you had a wife."

"Marry Mrs. Bransford?" Zeal gulped. He could feel the top of his bald head heating up. "I can't imagine where you'd get such a notion."

"Well, I declare. You don't have to fly off the handle at the mere mention of you getting a sweetheart. I've never seen a man so afraid of matrimony as you, Zeal."

"I'm not afraid—it's just not my calling. As the Apostle Paul said, *I say to the unmarried and widows, it is good for them if they abide even as I.*"

"Well, King Solomon said, *Two are better than one, because they have a good reward for their labor,*" Seraphim quoted as her counterargument. "*For if they fall, the one will lift up the other, but woe to him who is alone when he falleth, for he hath not another to help him up.*"

Zeal sighed. "It'd be a falsehood for me to claim I haven't had moments when I fretted over being alone in my old age. But I like my peace and quiet…" He looked down at the happy baby and grasped her tiny foot, rubbing the bottom of it with his thumb and watching her toes curl reflexively. "But who's to say? Maybe I won't always be alone, after all."

"I'd hate to see you get your hopes up, Brother. Chances are they'll find the baby's family, and they'll come and get her. Then, mark my words, this house will feel more lonely than ever."

"I only want what's best for Moses, be that with me or with her Mama or with some other loving family member. The letter we found in the fruit crate asked that I'd raise her so that she'd always know she's loved. So I'm just doing that for her, one day at a time. There is one thing I do know."

"What's that?"

"Every child should have a family."

"Amen to that, Brother."

374 Verbena Drive

Mo returned to the den with a bowl of popcorn resting on top of a fat photo album. "This is the story of your daddy," she said as she set the bowl on a coffee table and patted the bulging book with its red, faux leather cover. "It's got baby pictures and school certificates and homemade Mother's Day cards and newspaper clippings from his days on the track team."

Heidi was sitting on the sofa with one leg tucked under her. She had found the remote and turned off the television, then she had sat in nervous anticipation of what Mo might reveal to her about her father. Even though there were so many holes in her information about him, she drew some amount of comfort from filling in the holes herself, and these cold, hard facts might be worse than the fictional versions she had been creating in her mind all these years. Did she even want to know the truth?

Mo sat next to her and opened up the album. It felt strange and somehow forbidden for Heidi to see so many pictures of her dad. Once six-year old Heidi had left Mo and Poppy's house, her mom didn't want to talk about their life before the move. It wasn't as if she flat-out refused to discuss it. It was more of an unspoken agreement between them. A year later, and with the addition of her step-dad Chris, it was like her father and their old life had never existed.

"Your daddy was in the second grade in this picture," Mo said, squinting and pointing to a little boy in the front of a photo of three rows of sitting and standing children. "Boy-howdy, did he ever love that Fonzie shirt! For most of grade school, he always kept a comb in his back pocket to be just like The Fonz."

Though she had very few memories of him, Heidi recognized the same smile on the little boy which she remembered seeing on her young father's face. She also noticed that they shared a similar eye shape and color.

Mo turned more pages in the album, all while pointing out class-mates and highlighting awards and telling stories about Heidi's dad. After an hour, Heidi began to yawn, though she tried hard to fight it with the old acting trick of breathing through her nose.

Soon enough, Mo noticed her drowsiness and said, "We can comb through the rest of this tomorrow, honey. You look worn slap out, I'd say." Mo closed the book before Heidi could protest and set it on the coffee table. As she carried the empty popcorn bowl to the kitchen, she said, "I know it's bad for my bridgework, but I always like to chew on these unpopped kernels."

Heidi noticed a piece of paper folded into thirds on the floor under the coffee table. She assumed it must have fallen out of the album and leaned forward to pick it up. As Mo continued to talk from the kitchen describing a recent dentist appointment, Heidi unfolded the letter and read it.

Dear Mr. and Mrs. Seek,

I regret to inform you of the death of your son, Phillip C. Seek, Inmate #762745. His remains must be claimed within 48 hours or disposition must be made as provided by law.

We extend our sympathy in your loss.

"...but it doesn't matter that his hands are in your mouth and you can hardly swallow, let alone talk. The dentist still wants to ask you all manner of questions: *Any plans for the weekend, Mrs. Seek? You got any tomatoes in your garden this year, Mrs. Seek?* And on and on like that..." Mo was saying. As soon as she returned to the den, she saw Heidi holding the letter and sighed sadly. "Well, I was working up to that part, but I guess you were gonna hear it eventually."

Mo sat back down on the sofa and slowly pulled the letter from

Heidi's fingers. She refolded it and stuck it in the back of the album. "I don't need to look at it to know what it says. I have it memorized. We—me and your Poppy—read it so many times. Weeks after Phil died, I would find Poppy sitting in one of those chairs in the kitchen in the middle of the night. He said he would be dreaming about Phil—that he was alive and home—and then he would wake up and have to come out to the kitchen and find the letter to read it again to believe he was gone. It just didn't feel real."

"So what happened?" Heidi said in a whisper as she unconsciously leaned away from Mo. Her muscles were tense, as if she were bracing for a slap across her face.

"We never did get much by way of information. All the people at the prison would tell us was that he stepped in between two men who were fighting and got stabbed. They said he was just in the wrong place at the wrong time, like that was s'posed to be some kind of comfort to us or something we didn't already know. Your daddy invented being in the wrong place at the wrong time—and apparently kept on doing it up until his last breath."

"I didn't know—I mean, Mom said he died—of course, I knew that, but…" Heidi tried to examine the thoughts churning inside her: Disbelief? Shame? Confusion? Anger? An unsettling awareness that she had known it all along?

"You didn't know he died in prison?" Mo reached to grasp Heidi's hand. "I can't say I blame your Mama for leaving that part out. Phil was arrested just before she brought you here. I think she wanted to help him, at first, but then, when he got sentenced to 6-10 years… well, she had to start thinking of how to make a home for the two of you. She's a strong-willed woman, and sometimes strong people only want to move forward without ever looking back."

"I figured out that he had been in trouble, and I guessed a long time ago that he served some jail time." Heidi's voice got a fraction louder with every syllable. "But she said he was killed in a car accident. She said it was a slick road, and he was driving too fast on a curve. She said we couldn't go to the funeral, because there wasn't one."

"One of those things was true. We didn't have a funeral."

"She lied to me," Heidi groaned. "Everyone has just been lying to me all this time." Heidi realized that she had imagined the car accident scenario so often, she felt she had been there with her father, right next to him in the front seat, in his last moments. She could swear she knew exactly what the blurry windshield had looked like with the wipers passing back and forth furiously. The guard rail. The squeal of tires. The crunch of metal. The splintering of glass. "I need to know the truth—what really happened?"

"Your father had a problem with drugs. It got so bad that he started selling them so that he could afford to buy more. He got caught a few times early on and mainly had to pay a fine and spend a few months in jail, but the last time he got the book thrown at him. He was looking at years away from you and your Mama. While he was in there, he started figuring out that he'd let everybody down. He wrote us that he would do better, get better. He would study and get a degree. Come out a new man. Believe it or not, we felt like prison was an answer to prayer. It was too late for his marriage, but there was a chance he would stay clean and come out a better father for you."

"How long was he in prison before he was killed?" Heidi asked. She was trying to create a timeline. She needed concrete facts, details, dates. Something to organize in columns so that her thoughts weren't in such a jumble with her feelings.

"He died a few years after you moved with your Mama to Atlanta, so he had served about half of his sentence by then."

"What happened to the other people?" asked Heidi.

"What other people, honey?"

"The men who were fighting when he was stabbed."

"Well, why would you want to know that?" Mo asked, with concern in her voice.

"I have lived my whole life—26 years—with really no information about my father or even the chance to talk about him. I have to start somewhere."

"What good would it do to know about that now? We can't change any of it. Let's just concentrate on the good parts," said Mo as she pointed to the photo album. "You have your whole life ahead of you. Don't let this misery ruin everything that's good."

"You said my Mom is a strong woman. Well, I don't know that I've ever felt strong and maybe all of these secrets are part of the reason why. But I think a strong person doesn't ignore the bad parts and act like they never happened. A strong person looks for answers."

Morgan's Hat, Tennessee, 1941

When Sunday morning came, Tillie realized that Pastor Cooley had never contacted her. She assumed his sister Seraphim must have provided the assistance with the baby which he was expecting. Tillie's real question was whether or not Zeal had had time to read the sermon she had typed for him to preach. Would he be angry about how far she had strayed from his original instructions?

Tillie always arrived at the church at least an hour before services to be sure everything was in order, and it was a good thing she did, too. Most of the parishioners of Berea Baptist had no idea of the catastrophes she had prevented and the messes she had cleaned up before they strolled in at 10:00 a.m. There had been busted pipes in the middle of winter and spoiled food left out after a summer wedding. Tillie never ceased to be amazed by how many animals chose to crawl, fly, or slither into the sanctuary to experience their final moments on earth. Imagining their magnetic pull to God's house and its sacred altar would be a beautiful sentiment to ruminate upon if it weren't for the pronounced stench their decaying bodies could produce over a weekend.

As she straightened the stack of printed bulletins by the door, Tillie felt a line of perspiration form along her upper lip. She was nervous. As she dressed for services, she had rehearsed what she would say in defense of the sermon she wrote. Even with this preparation, Tillie couldn't still the fluttering feeling she felt in her chest.

Zeal arrived with Seraphim and Moses only five minutes prior to the start of service. Tillie was waiting for him on the front steps and greeting church folks as they walked inside.

"I was about to send a couple of deacons over to fetch you, Pastor," Tillie whispered as she ushered Zeal to the foyer. "Do you have your sermon?"

Zeal pulled a jumble of notecards from his inside coat pocket. "Yes! I've got them right here." He watched Seraphim as she carried Moses and sat down on the front pew, saying, "Good morning," to the ladies who stopped by to *oooh* and *ahhh* over the baby. "Trials and tribulations!" Zeal said. "We had a difficult night! Moses was suffering greatly from gas of the bowels. Nothing would soothe her."

Tillie used a Kleenex to wipe a blob of spit-up from Zeal's shoulder and fixed his wayward collar. "So you read over the sermon?" she asked without looking him in the eye, preferring to concentrate on plucking a nearly invisible ball of fluff from his sleeve.

"No. I never had a chance to, but not to worry," Zeal said as he held his Bible aloft victoriously. "I can preach with my eyes closed, if needs be."

The organist began playing "All Hail the Power of Jesus' Name," and the congregation stood and joined in. Zeal hustled to the front, and Tillie sat in her regular spot near the back of the sanctuary. She took a piece of hard candy from her purse, unwrapped it, and popped it in her mouth. Her nervousness was so heightened, she had to remind herself to smile and nod at those sitting around her.

"And crown Him Lord of all!" the congregation sang together as they finished the opening song. Zeal stood behind the podium and took the cards from his pocket. "Good morning and welcome to the Lord's House at Berea Baptist church!" he said enthusiastically. "Open up your Bibles to the book of Haggai…" Zeal's brow furrowed as he flipped through the cards. Someone coughed and a mother shushed her two sons as Pastor Cooley opened his Bible and took out the typed pages, skimming them quickly before beginning. "I used to work at my Uncle Uriah's funeral parlor," he read aloud. "Maybe I've told some of you about it…I did a bit of everything at that funeral parlor—arranging the flowers, laying out the bodies, even some of the hair and makeup work. It turned out that it wasn't the right job for me. I preferred helping the living, instead of working with the dead. Oh sure, working at a funeral home is helping the families of the dead, but I still felt a different calling for my life."

Zeal stopped and glanced at the back of the room where Tillie sat. She smiled feebly and sucked vigorously on her candy.

"But ya'll know what a dead body is like. Stiff and rotting. Useless, really. Only thing left to do with a dead loved one is to clean him up and have a funeral. Well, this is the scene Christ comes upon in the Book of John, chapter 11. It's his friend Lazarus who's died. His sisters are crying and mad that he didn't get there sooner, and the body is already wrapped up in burial cloths and decaying. It's over. But we see more to the story, because Christ had a powerful plan for their suffering."

Along with the rest of Tillie's words, Zeal read from the Bible passage. He finished by saying, "Verse 45 says, *Then many of the Jews which came to Mary, and had seen the things which Jesus did, believed on him.* Brothers and sisters, I ask you to do the same. Remember the good things Jesus has done as you go through your week. Amen."

As the organist began playing the invitation song, Zeal made a beeline down the aisle to the foyer, gesturing with a quick movement of his head for Tillie to join him there. "Mrs. Bransford," Zeal whispered just loud enough for Tillie to hear him over the congregational singing. "This isn't…why did you…when I asked you…*Haggai*?" Though he couldn't cobble together the right words to construct a sentence, Tillie had no trouble understanding him.

"I'm sorry, Pastor," Tillie answered. "I know this wasn't what you asked me to do. I just wanted you to see a different way of preaching to your flock, something a little more personal. You're so skilled at talking to church people one-on-one, but your sermons tend to be… well, drab and full of fancy words. Pastor, some of these people can't read, let alone understand the things you learned in seminary. You've had an interesting life. Why not preach on it?" Tillie adjusted her glasses as they slid down her sweaty nose. "I was just trying to help."

"Well, I would prefer you didn't offer that kind of help to me again," he spat out. Tillie had never heard notes of rage in Zeal's tone before.

"I am sorry. I don't know what else to say."

The parishioners were beginning to leave the church in large and small groups. They each stopped to briefly visit with Zeal before heading on to their dinners.

"Wonderful sermon, Pastor!" exclaimed Deacon Foster.

"I was so touched by your reading of the Scriptures," his wife Birdie added. "Lazarus, come forth!" Birdie wiped her nose with a lacy handkerchief. "Stirring!"

"Thank you," Zeal murmured and shook the church deacon's hand. "Have a blessed Sunday, folks."

"You 'bout had us all fooled with your opening words about Haggai!" said Sheriff Brown with his wife Hazel on his arm. "Glad to be back in the New Testament!"

"All of Scripture is inspired of God and profitable for our correction and instruction in righteousness, Ish," Zeal cautioned.

"Yessir," Sheriff Brown responded, sheepishly. "Well, it was a good sermon, anyhow."

Tillie looked on as the people spoke to Zeal about the sermon, *her* sermon. She felt a mixture of delight and regret. She knew Zeal was suffering, but Tillie did find solace in the fact that only she knew the source of his suffering. As far as the rest of Berea Baptist knew, their beloved pastor had written the sermon, and that was enough for them.

"Good morning, Mrs. Bransford."

Tillie was pulled from her thoughts by the voice of a woman standing behind her.

"Oh, Mrs. Putnam! I hope you're doing well."

"I'm fine...just fine." Marjorie Putnam glanced over Tillie's shoulder and spied Seraphim holding little Moses. "Everybody's talking about that baby ya'll found here at the church. I was wondering... did that have anything to do with our little talk the other day about Miss Willadeene Lathrop and her kin?"

A tiny piece of the hard candy still lingered in Tillie's mouth. She pressed it against her cheek as she weighed her words. How much did this gossipmonger need to know? Might she be helpful to Tillie in her quest to flesh out the unknown names on the recipe cards? "How about I drop by this afternoon and fill you in on a few things?" Tillie answered surreptitiously.

They made their plans, and Marjorie left the building. Tillie gave one last wave as she watched her leave and thought about how she would reveal as little as possible about Moses while simultaneously milking every bit of pertinent information from that woman until Marjorie Putnam was tapped dry. She may have disappointed Pastor Cooley with the sermon she wrote, but Tillie was determined to find out the identity of the elusive Miss A.

374 Verbena Drive

Heidi couldn't sleep. She lay on top of the covers on the bed in the spare room and randomly selected from the various ideas emerging into her confused thoughts. Questions eddied and churned in her mind like a tornado. She was reminded of the scene in *The Wizard of Oz*, where Dorothy looks out the window to see a cow floating by and a knitting woman in a rocking chair and two men in a rowboat, all while her own house is spinning. Trying to put her finger on the most pressing emotion boiling inside her—anger, frustration, dizziness, restlessness—she decided to act.

Heidi opened her laptop and typed in the date and place listed on the letter from the prison. In a few clicks, she found a short newspaper article about the incident. "The Kentucky Department of Corrections is investigating the death of an inmate which occurred last month. The cause and manner of death have been identified in conjunction with the results of an autopsy and an investigation, a KDOC spokeswoman said Monday. 'We have contacted family members of the deceased, Phillip C. Seek. The victim was pronounced dead in the prison hospital after succumbing to his wounds,' the spokeswoman said. Further investigations reveal that the deceased was defending a fellow prisoner at the time of the attack."

Heidi continued to launch new searches. She scribbled notes on a pad of paper she had found in the kitchen. She uncovered disturbing articles about deplorable prison facilities and inhumane treatment of inmates. There were websites full of stories just like Mo's with other family members receiving the same indifferent letters, emails, and even curt messages on answering machines announcing the unexpected death of their loved ones while in custody.

She found a long-abandoned online message board started by families of inmates from the same prison as the one where her dad had been. She scrolled through posts—mostly questions which went unanswered—and found one from 2002.

> My son's name is Jason. I'm looking for the family of the man who died because he was helping my son. The man's name was Phil Seek. I just want to say thank you to them.
>
> –Linda

Heidi shut her laptop and stared at the wall. Then she checked the time, almost 2:00 a.m. She needed to talk to someone, so she took a chance that Josh was still awake in L.A.

"Hello?" he answered.

"Hey, Josh. It's me."

"I know it's you. What's going on? You never stay up this late. Is everything okay?"

"Not really," Heidi answered honestly. She told Josh about the photo album and Mo's letter from the prison. "Now I find this message board and this woman, Linda. Do I answer it? Would she even respond? It was from so long ago, maybe she doesn't get alerts for this board anymore."

"Answer it," Josh replied. "What can it hurt? Just don't sign it Heidi Phillips."

"Right…right." Heidi opened her laptop and stared at the post again. She set the phone on the bed and began typing. Then she picked up the phone and said, "Okay, so I wrote, 'I think you are talking about my dad. Please contact me. –Heidi' Then I put my old email, that AOL one that I had in high school. What do you think?"

"I think you're about to deep-dive into a rabbit hole searching for Lindas and Jasons in a 500-mile radius of where you're sitting instead of going to sleep."

Heidi smiled. "You know me too well."

"Call me tomorrow," said Josh. "I hope you hear something from Linda."

"Thanks. Me too."

"But seriously…try to get some sleep. I love you."

"Love you, too. Good night."

Heidi decided Josh was right, and she closed her laptop. She wrote the name LINDA in her notes and circled it, then set both the pad of paper and the laptop on the nightstand. She turned off the lamp and suddenly felt downright exhausted. Compared to the anxiety she had felt a few hours before, this bone-tired fatigue was heavenly. Her last thought just before drifting off to sleep was a long dormant memory resurfacing out of somewhere deep in her subconscious.

In the memory, Heidi was perched on the sofa in the den of that very house, feet dangling under a Minnie Mouse fleece blanket. She was sitting beside Mo, eating popcorn and watching *The Wizard of Oz* on the television. Each time the Wicked Witch of the West came on the screen, Heidi would hide her face under the blanket, and Mo would hold her hand.

"I'll tell you when that mean, old witch is gone, honey. Don't you worry," Mo told her. "I'd do anything for my baby girl 'cuz I love you from here to the hereafter and ten miles past that."

Morgan's Hat, Tennessee, 1941

After a light lunch following Sunday services, Tillie made her way to the southside of town and the Putnam family home, a structure originally purchased as much for its layout and basic amenities as it was for its view of a major thoroughfare leading into the town square. When Tillie pulled up in her Plymouth in front of Marjorie's house, Mrs. Putnam was sitting in a rocking chair on her porch, watching the bustle of people passing by on their Sunday drives. "Mrs. Bransford! Come on up!" she called.

Her excitement about receiving some juicy pieces of gossip was evident to Tillie. She could see that Marjorie couldn't get her talking fast enough, but Tillie was prepared. After all, she was one of the founding members of the Davis County League of Church Secretaries and the author of their pledge to "uphold the standards of conduct and confidentiality befitting those granted the momentous task of serving my Lord and His church," which they recited at every meeting.

"Your goldenrod and cardinal lobelias sure look pretty," Tillie remarked coolly, gesturing to the yellow and red spiky flowers in the pots by the steps.

"Yes…well, thank you, but…" Marjorie began.

"It's always sad to see the summer beauties dry up, but the autumn months still have lots to offer if you're willing to look for it." Tillie enjoyed dangling a mouse in front of this cat.

"I'm sure that is true." Marjorie gestured to the rocking chair next to her. "Now sit down and tell me what all you've heard. I know you visited Ophelia Gautreaux up on Harley Hill…" she prompted.

"Lovely woman, and that house! A feat of Victorian architecture! Can you imagine living in a mansion with actual towers? It would be like being a princess in a fairy tale!"

"Yes, yes…lovely…and you found out…" She paused, waiting for Tillie to finish the thought.

"Mrs. Gautreaux gave me this." Tillie opened her boxy purple handbag and took out the recipe box.

"Oh." Marjorie sounded disappointed.

"It's an old recipe box. I believe it used to belong to Miss Willadeene." She opened the box and flipped through the recipe cards. "Here's Norma Peter's recipe for Prune Pudding. Isn't that just delightful?"

"If you like that sort of thing," Marjorie answered coolly.

"I was thinking about typing up the recipes to make a cookbook—a Berea Baptist cookbook—though I'm sure we'd also get recipes from folks outside of our congregation. We could print them and sell them to raise money to help pay for chairs and tables and such for the new Sunday School classrooms. What do you think?"

Marjorie sighed. "That sounds like a perfectly fine idea," she replied with a tinge of frustrated resignation in her voice. "So you didn't find out anything about that baby's kin?"

"Oh! Did you think I came here to chinwag about that poor child? Heavens, Mrs. Putnam! What a thing to imagine I'd do! You know what the Pastor says about gossiping: *Where there's no wood, the fire goes out!*"

"So you came here just to show me this old recipe box?"

"Well, I thought you could help me with the project, gather more recipes and so on. Also I had questions about a few of these cards. I know most of the people, but there were some—five, to be precise—whose names I didn't recognize. I wouldn't want to include those recipes in our cookbook, only to find out that they're written by bootleggers or horse-thieves or some other bad sort."

"Horse-thieves are known to do a lot of baking, are they?" Marjorie asked sarcastically.

"Anyhow, I have only lived in Morgan's Hat since my husband died, and you are acquainted with so many people in town, being born and bred here. You are known to be quite a notable figure in these parts, a mother to many and a friend to all."

Marjorie sat a little straighter and smiled smugly. "Show me what you've got, Mrs. Bransford."

Tillie pulled out five cards and read off the names: "Jam Layer Cake from Royal L. Whitman. Tomato Aspic from Olivia Simpson. Get Well Soon Chicken Soup from B.L. Waddle. Hawaiian Wedding Cake from Tabitha Langford. And the last one is Irene Marley's Railroad Pie." She handed the cards to Marjorie and asked, "Do you know these women?"

"I recognize all the names, except B.L. Waddle. Oh, I bet that's Bennie Lee Waddle. She used to be the schoolteacher here. Spinster lady from Alabama. Then there's Royal Whitman. Royal moved to Memphis and eventually died of the grip. Sad. I can't recall what her connection was with Morgan's Hat. Irene Marley used to be neighbors with my cousin. She lived to be in her 90s, I believe. She had a passel of sons who cared for her up until the end." Marjorie stopped to take a breath before continuing. "Olivia Simpson…now, that's a name I haven't seen in a while. She moved away ages ago. Unless I'm mistaken, she was some kind of kin to Miss Willadeene. Then…let's see…The name Tabitha Langford may not be familiar to you, but that's because she married Rev. Hoffman soon after you came to Morgan's Hat. She's the one and only Bitty Hoffman, Queen of the Christmas Pageant at the Methodist church. Bitty'd be pleasant to be around if she weren't so tightfisted. She wouldn't give a nickel to see Jesus riding a bicycle!"

"Well, I so appreciate your help, Mrs. Putnam!" said Tillie. "You've been such a dear and a true friend of the church!" She gathered the cards and placed them back in the box. "I better get to typing these up!"

"Thanks for stopping by, Mrs. Bransford. It was real nice visiting with you. I'll look through my tried and true recipes this week and bring some over to church for your cookbook. Come to think of it, I have a real nice Jell-O salad recipe using R.C. Cola and cherry pie

filling that I always make for the Independence Day picnic. People seemed to like it."

As she drove her Plymouth away from Marjorie's house, Tillie reflected on their visit and was pleased. She felt optimistic about the information Marjorie had given her, but she wasn't ready to go home just yet.

Though she normally set aside Sunday evenings for personal time—sitting in her front room, listening to her favorite radio programs and eating a Milky Way—Tillie drove to the church. She parked in front but stayed in her car, looking over at the pastorium. She saw Zeal standing in the doorway, holding Moses and waving goodbye to Seraphim and her son Leonard as they drove away.

Tillie decided she needed to make amends with Zeal before work on Monday morning, so she walked over to his little house and knocked on the door.

"Oh, come in, Mrs. Bransford," Zeal replied when he saw her. "After the events of this morning, I believe we need to talk."

Tillie stepped just inside the living room and kept her left hand on the handles of her handbag hanging from her right arm. She stood stiffly, breathing deeply through her nose, ready to absorb the censure she knew was coming.

"I had a long talk with Sera." Zeal transferred Moses to her preferred sideways position and swung her gently from side to side. "And now I feel like I should apologize."

"Apologize?"

"Yes. I lost my temper, and I'm sorry. I could blame the sleepless nights and the toil from caring for a newborn, but I won't make excuses for my bad behavior."

Tillie was stunned. "I am the one who should apologize, Pastor..." she began.

"You were just trying to help me, and my pride got the better of me. As the Good Book says, *Pride goeth before destruction, and a haughty spirit before a fall.* I could see that the congregation sat up and listened better to the sermon you wrote than any I'd ever done."

"Well, I shouldn't have gone against your wishes. I promise it won't happen again."

Zeal laid the sleeping baby in the fruit crate. "I'd be grateful—if you had the time, that is—I would truly appreciate it if you were to do the same for next Sunday, too," he responded without looking at Tillie. He brushed the whisps of fine hair from Moses' forehead. "I've been writing sermons the same way for more than thirty years. Seems as if I need guidance in constructing a sermon that has...as Sera put it... more heart and less head."

"I would be happy to help any way that I can," Tillie answered, still a little shocked. She was about to turn and leave, then she said, "Oh, I wanted to ask you a question, if you have a second." She reached in her handbag and pulled out the recipe box, lifting one of the cards from the box. "Do you happen to remember Olivia Simpson? I was told she lived here years ago, but she might be family to Willadeene Lathrop. I was just looking to see if she might be a clue to the identity of Miss A, little Moses' mama."

Zeal hesitated for a moment before answering. Tillie thought she saw a slight change in his expression, something fleeting across his eyes. "Olivia Simpson lived with Miss Willadeene for a piece of time. She was a kind of companion to her back when the Lathrop house was home to large social gatherings—Easter egg hunts and Christmas eggnog parties. But she wasn't kin to Miss Willadeene, just a close family friend."

"I have this notion...well, I wonder if there's a connection between Miss A and Olivia Simpson. I can't help thinking that Olivia went on to have children after she moved away, and perhaps her daughter would come back for visits at the Lathrop Mansion."

"Olivia Simpson lived in Morgan's Hat for a short piece of time. She left while I was in seminary. A few years after I came back here to preach, I heard news that she had died of tuberculosis."

"Do you know if she ever had any children?" asked Tillie in almost a whisper as she attempted to match the volume of Zeal's low voice.

"I couldn't say." Zeal shoved his hands in his pockets and trained his eye on a stain on the faded rug under his feet.

"I had another thought," Tillie began when she realized that Zeal wouldn't offer any more details about Miss Simpson. "Royal Whitman's name was listed on the recipe cards. Mrs. Putnam said she moved to Memphis. That got me thinking, maybe Memphis is a clue." She pointed to the bold lettering on the side of the fruit crate: PHARAOH ORCHARDS OF MEMPHIS.

"Call Silas Padgett tomorrow and see if he's missing any fruit crates," he suggested.

"That's a good idea. Moreover, I believe I'll try to find out if there are any music schools in Memphis."

"I hate for you to feel like you're wasting your time hunting, especially if it all turns out to be a wild goose chase," said Zeal. "We have so little to go on."

"I really don't mind doing it," Tillie responded cheerfully. "As I've been searching for answers, I've begun to worry about our Miss A: Where is she? How is she doing? Is she sad or lonely? It feels like I'm hunting for gold at the end of a rainbow. Family would be a treasure for both lost souls."

Zeal's eyes met Tillie's, and he smiled. "I'm having a plate of beans and leftover cornbread for supper. It's a meager meal, but I'd be happy to share it with you, if you'd like to join me," Zeal offered.

Tillie looked at the little man standing in his sock feet. She noticed that one of his big toes stuck out of a hole in his sock. "No," she said, fighting the urge to pull the sock right off his foot and sew it up. "But thank you. I'm going to drop something off at the office and head home."

"I see. Well, good evening, Mrs. Bransford."

"Evening, Pastor."

374 Verbena Drive

As soon as Heidi woke up early the next morning, she automatically reached for her laptop and checked the chat room where she had found Linda, Jason's mom. She was hopeful that Jason could shed light on the circumstances surrounding her father's death. She also wanted to know more about the man himself, what her dad was like and was he really committed to changing while serving his prison sentence. What could have her relationship with her dad been like if things had ended differently?

Her laptop powered on, and she found the bookmarked website quickly. No reply to her comment. She switched to her old email and found no new messages. Heidi shut the laptop and slid out of bed. She tiptoed across the hall to the bathroom. The house was quiet and still. She heard only the hum of the refrigerator coming from the kitchen.

Walking in her bare feet, Heidi crept into the kitchen to make a cup of coffee. She looked all over the counter and inside the cabinets, but found no coffee machine, percolator, or French press. All she could scrounge up was a teakettle and an old tin with the label: *General Foods International Coffee Suisse Mocha*. She opened the tin and found the contents had solidified into a concrete lump at the bottom. Craving coffee now more than ever, she decided to grab her keys and drive to the closest McDonald's.

"Heidi? You alright, honey?" Mo came out of her bedroom. "I thought you'd sleep later. You looked so tired last night."

"I'm feeling fine," Heidi explained. "Actually, I slept great last night. I was just going to run out and get some coffee."

Mo looked at the tin box and teakettle. "I'm so sorry I don't have any coffee. I've never liked the stuff myself, but if I'd-a known you were coming—"

"Oh, don't worry about it! I'm totally fine going out and getting some. Do you want anything? Maybe a McMuffin or something?"

Mo thought for a moment. "I wouldn't turn away some of those hotcakes."

Heidi backed out of the driveway, turned right at the light, and headed out of the residential neighborhood and into an area with stores, gas stations, and a small hospital. She pulled into the drive-thru lane and shouted her order into the speaker. "Hey, I need an order of hotcakes and a large coffee." She pulled around to the first window to pay.

"That's $5.97," said the woman sitting on the other side of the window. She barely looked up as Heidi handed her a ten-dollar bill. After she had pulled out the coins and bills for her change, the woman finally looked at her customer. "Wait, I know you...don't I?"

Heidi blushed, wishing she could hide behind the sunglasses she had accidentally broken on Mo's front porch. "I don't think so," Heidi responded with her open hand still waiting for her change.

"No, seriously," said the woman. "I know you. Are you from here?"

"No. I'm just visiting my grandmother."

"Hang on...I know I've seen you before! Oh, I got it...say: 'Cracks in your foundation? How unsettling! Call us. We're the Crack Doctors!'"

Heidi chuckled uncomfortably, then sighed. "Yeah, that was me." She weighed her current options, considering how rude it would be to just drive away without her money or her food.

"That commercial used to come on all the time! You're Heidi Phillips, right?"

"Yep."

"Of course, you used to be Heidi Seek, though. You probably don't remember me, but we were in the same kindergarten class—Mrs. James?"

"Oh…oh, yeah. I'm sorry I didn't recognize you."

"No worries. There's no reason why you would. I'm Jessica, by the way."

"Jessica…it's great to see you again."

"I came over to your house a few times that year. Growing up in my house, we never had much of anything homemade to eat—mostly Little Debbie cakes, stuff like that, but I remember your grandma made these really thick sugar cookies."

"That's right! We had a tea party!" It was all coming back to Heidi—the tiny cups and saucers, the cloth napkins on their laps, and Mo's old Easter Sunday hats perched on their five-year-old heads.

"I remember I spilled hot tea all over the table. I can still see that white tablecloth covered in a big, brown puddle. In my house, that would've gotten you a slap, but your grandma was so sweet about it." Jessica smiled at the memory. "I saw you on those episodes of *Days of Our Lives*. You were great! It's too bad they killed you off during that zombie attack. But, who knows? Maybe they'll bring you back as Storm Sylvester's twin sister. So, are you here to film something?"

"No. I'm just visiting Mo." The driver in line behind Heidi honked his horn.

Jessica stuck her head out of the window and cut her eyes at him before saying, "Well, I'm so glad I got to see you, Heidi. Tell your grandma I said *hi*." She gave Heidi her change.

"I will! Bye!" Heidi stopped at the next window to get her food and drove back to Mo's house.

During the entire drive to McDonald's, all she could think about was the chat room and Linda and Jason. She had wondered why this quest had become so important to her. Anything she learned about her father wouldn't change the fact that he was gone or that he hadn't been there for her when it had mattered.

But on the drive back, she replayed the decades-old memory of Jessica and the tea party. For the first time, Heidi attempted to think about her childhood from Mo's perspective. Was she glad to take care of Heidi that year? Or was it hassle to look after a five-year-old? Was Mo relieved when Heidi's mom picked her up, or was she disappointed to see her go? She decided that whatever, if

anything, that she might learn from Jason, she would be grateful for that part of her childhood. Because the more she thought about it, the more she realized how much Mo had to set aside her own worry and heartache that year. She and Poppy had been asked to raise a granddaughter while enduring the fear and disappointment of knowing their only son was in prison. It must've been an arduous, daily undertaking just to get up and face another day.

"Mo! I'm back!" Heidi yelled as soon as she entered the house. She set a bag with Mo's food on the kitchen counter and took her coffee into the spare room. She inhaled deeply and opened her laptop again, silently praying for a response. She only saw her own post. She reread it:

```
I think you are talking about my dad.
Please contact me.
```

Heidi took a hot swig from her coffee and checked her email. She was stunned to see she had one new message. It said,

```
Dear Heidi, I can't believe you answered
my post in the prison chat room. It's
been so long, and so much has happened
since I first wrote that. I asked Jason
this morning and he said it was OK for
me to send you his phone number. He is
excited to talk to you about your dad.
God bless you!
```

Heidi read the message through three times. She picked up her cell phone and began to dial the number Linda had listed in the email, but stopped midway through.

Instead, she copied the number on her pad of paper, then took her coffee and stepped back out into the hall. Mo's bedroom door was opened, but Heidi called out before going in. "Mo? Is it okay if I come in?" she asked.

"Of course, honey. I'm just tending to my babies." Mo had a long, narrow table pushed up against the window on the other side of her bed. It was covered with a variety of potted plants. "Your Poppy wasn't much of a fan of having plants indoors. He thought all of the growing should be done outdoors, so when I lost him, I started my collection." She tugged at the curved stem of a wilted, brown leaf until it was freed from its plant. Then she added the leaf to a small pile.

Heidi set her coffee cup on the tall bureau by the door and joined Mo to stand by the various vines, leaves, and blooms. "They're gorgeous."

"Thanks, honey. Let me introduce you to them. Girls, this is my granddaughter Heidi. She's the one I've been telling you about. Heidi, this one is called a Flaming Katy, and this is a Purple Shamrock. This is a pretty common one but still a beauty—it's a Rattlesnake Plant. See the stripes? And do you know what this one is called?"

Heidi shook her head.

"It's called a Prayer Plant. They call it that because it looks like it folds its hands to pray at night."

"Why do you grow them in here, in your bedroom?" Heidi asked.

"There's lots to know if you want to take care of these plants, especially since most are tropical so they're not from 'round here. They all need different soil and food. Some even have to stay in the dark for a few days during the colder months or they won't bloom again. As far as light goes, these lovely ladies need an east-facing window. Take these Moth Orchids, for instance. They love it when it's bright but not too hot." Mo gently cupped the delicate, white bloom in her hand. "This window seems to be just right, I reckon." Mo set a miniature watering can on the floor and began to make her bed.

"Oh, I'll help," said Heidi as she strode to the other side of the bed and pulled the sheet tight.

Mo smiled. "It sure has been nice having you here. If I was an orchid I'd say you're just the right amount of sunshine for me." They finished making the bed, and Mo asked, "How are you feeling after our talk last night? I couldn't sleep myself for thinking that I sprung a lot of bad stuff on you."

Heidi sat on the edge of the bed and Mo joined her. She told her grandmother about the chat room and Linda giving her Jason's number.

"So are you going to call him?" Mo asked.

"I don't know," Heidi answered. "What do you think?"

"Well, I found my peace years ago, but you need to do what you think is best. Poppy would probably say that you're liable to open up a can of worms, but I daresay he would've liked to have more of the story."

"I'm just so afraid. What if Jason lies to me? What if this isn't even about my dad? What if the things he tells me makes me miss my dad more or even hate him?"

Mo squeezed Heidi's hand. "You know, I never understood people saying, *Open up a can of worms*, like it was a bad thing. Poppy loved to go fishing with some of his friends when he was healthy. He even took me out once, but I just couldn't see the fun in it—getting up early just to sit in a boat without talking. Anyhow, one thing I learned was that there are some times when you need to open up a can of worms if you want to catch a big one."

Mo stood up to head into the kitchen. Heidi followed, but stopped to grab her coffee cup from the bureau. She noticed a pair of clip-on earrings made to look like dangling clusters of grapes, each purple stone wired to another. Heidi picked them up from the delicate china saucer where they sat.

"Pretty aren't they? I never could wear clip-ons though. Hurt my ears too much. They're yours if you want them," said Mo.

"No. I couldn't—" Heidi began.

"Take them, honey. They've just been sitting there forever."

"But even if you don't wear them, you must like looking at them."

The earrings sat in the palm of Heidi's hand. Mo brushed her finger across the faux gems and gazed at them with a look of affection rarely bestowed on costume jewelry.

"There are some things that you don't have to see every day to remember in here." Mo tapped her own chest. "Take them, Doll Baby. I want you to," she said as she folded Heidi's fingers over the earrings.

"Only if you're sure—" Heidi began.

"I'm sure. Anyhow, I seem to remember that purple is your favorite color, or leastwise, it used to be. I remember because we had that in common." Mo winked at Heidi, before leaving the bedroom in search of fast food hotcakes.

Heidi smiled, then carried the earrings into the spare room and dropped them into her Gucci handbag.

Morgan's Hat, Tennessee, 1941

On Monday morning, Tillie arrived at the church building at her regular time. She peeked inside Zeal's private office but found it dark and empty. Tillie wondered if she should check in on him at home to see if Zeal needed any help, but she suddenly felt her cheeks flush at the memory of his toe sticking out of his brown argyle socks and decided against it.

She sat down at her desk and picked up the phone receiver. "Morning, Prissy," Tillie said as soon as the operator came on the line. "Do you have time to look up something for me?" Tillie explained that she was searching for a telephone number of a music school in Memphis.

Tillie could hear the switchboard operator grunt slightly as she reached for a telephone book, followed by a dull thud and the sound of pages flipping.

"What's the name of the school?" Prissy asked.

"Well, I don't exactly know the name of the school. I was hoping you could find the name of any music schools in the area and then connect me to them." Tillie doodled in the corner of her date book as she waited for Prissy's forced reply.

As a rule, Tillie preferred to communicate face-to-face, so she didn't enjoy talking on the telephone. Communicating in this way, she felt blindfolded. She was unable to compliment Prissy on her new dress or her Jell-O salad mold or her darling hairdo or her embroidered throw pillows or her children's good behavior. She always felt it was more difficult to win people over when she couldn't read their expressions and adjust the conversation accordingly.

"I'll need to do some digging. I'll call you back." The brusque switchboard operator hung up the line without further explanation. Prissy's abrupt nature was so contradictory to her own that Tillie could only sit in dejected silence. She had heard that the telephone operators in other counties were known to be pleasant and talkative, such as the one two counties over who would call up townspeople to sing to them for their birthdays and another one who could make up rhymes on the spot to communicate a particular message—

Aunt Gladys called to say she's coming soon.

She's also bringing your cousin June.

But Prissy was a different type altogether.

After rousing her spirits with a piece of hard candy from the stash she kept in one of her desk drawers, Tillie grabbed her handbag and made her way out to her Plymouth. She drove to the town square, parking in one of the spaces near Padgett's Grocery store.

The bell above the door jingled as she entered. Joyce Padgett, co-owner of the store along with her husband Silas, was standing behind the counter scrutinizing the contents of a form with a pencil clamped between her teeth.

"Good morning, Mrs. Bransford!" she called as Tillie approached the counter.

"Good morning!" Tillie's mood instantly brightened, and she was encouraged by Joyce's pleasant greeting and its assurance that some people still knew how to be sociable. "I was wondering if I could ask you a quick question."

"Of course," said Joyce as she set her pencil down. "I'll do my best!"

"I was wondering if you have any fruit coming in from Memphis, perhaps from a place called Pharaoh Orchards."

Joyce pulled a large ledger from under the counter and began looking through the pages, all while saying things like, *hmm* and *well*. Eventually, she shut the book and said, "I don't believe we get any of our produce from Memphis, and I've not heard of a place called Pharaoh Orchards."

Tillie's shoulders slumped. She wasn't sure what she had expected to hear. If it had been one of the crates from Padgett's Grocery, it wouldn't necessarily prove anything. But maybe it would indicate that Moses' mother was a local woman, one who had been around the store and Joyce might remember seeing. Was it likely that Miss A would carry her baby in a fruit crate all the way from Memphis? It may be far-fetched, but it was one of the few leads at her disposal which she could follow.

"Is there something else I can help you with? Are you needing some fruits and vegetables? Or maybe this is to do with that sweet baby Pastor Cooley is looking after? She can't already be out of the powdered milk you bought her."

"No, I believe Pastor has all that he needs at the moment." Tillie looked around at the store and saw that no shoppers were in earshot. "To be honest, Mrs. Padgett, I'm trying to locate the baby's mother. The little darling was left in a fruit crate, and I thought if I could learn more about the orchard on the crate label—"

"You thought it would lead you to the mama," said Joyce, finishing Tillie's thought. Joyce shook her head. "That mama must've been suffering and in a tight spot. It would be mighty hard to leave your baby. When my girl was a newborn, I had a hard enough time leaving her with my own mother when it was time for me to come in and do a bit of bookkeeping for the store."

"How is Adell? I haven't seen her in a while."

"Oh, she's gone to live with my sister. Ever since she got her first girdle, she's been preening around for the boys in this town entirely too much for my liking…and especially for the liking of Mr. Padgett." Joyce withdrew a rag from her apron pocket and began wiping the perfectly clean wooden counter. "Generally, I reckon fathers have a hard time with daughters when they get to a certain age. They just don't know what to make of them, but when you add on that this one is headstrong and wants to play music *on stage* for a living…well, ordinary, decent people just can't make heads nor tails of daughters like them."

Tillie involuntarily took a step back before responding. "I forgot all about Adell's talents on the piano. Every time I heard her play, I came away thinking she was mighty gifted. Where did you say she's living?"

"With my sister in Kentucky."

"Is she in school there?" asked Tillie.

"No. Adell finished up at the grammar school here, but we decided further schooling wasn't much use for her." Joyce dropped her voice to a whisper. "I love her to death, but she hasn't got the sense God gave a goose."

"Well, thank you for your time, Mrs. Padgett," said Tillie.

"No trouble at all. Oh, and I wanted to let you know that we're getting in more talcum powder today, if you think the little lamb might need some. I know we were out when you came in before."

"That's very thoughtful. I'll stop by later. Good-bye."

Tillie drove back to the church building, her mind full of speculations and musings. She considered going over to Zeal's house to re-read the letter Moses' mother had tucked inside the folds of Moses' blanket in the fruit crate, but decided she would rather sit by the phone, waiting for Prissy to call her back.

She entered the office and sat down at her desk, staring at the phone to will it into ringing. After admitting her foolishness, she took the cover off her typewriter and threaded a sheet of typing paper through the rollers. Tillie tried to decide on a subject for Zeal's next sermon, but all she could think of was the likelihood that Adell Padgett was Miss A, Moses' mother. The Padgetts didn't attend Berea Baptist, but were regular attendees at the Methodist church. Still, she could've visited on a Sunday when Zeal preached about the woman bathing Jesus' feet. But Adell was only sixteen or seventeen, altogether too young to have been been alive when Zeal preached about the Sinful Woman in 1922. Maybe it wasn't as long ago as Tillie assumed, and she got the date wrong, or perhaps he preached on it again more recently. As a rule, Zeal didn't like to repeat sermons, but after 30 years, it just couldn't be helped.

She stood to re-examine his past sermons in the filing cabinet just as the phone rang.

"Hello," Tillie answered.

"This is the switchboard. I looked into your question," said Prissy. "There aren't any music schools in Memphis, least none listed in any directories I can lay my hands on."

"Oh, well, thank you," said Tillie, disappointed.

"Anything else I can help you with? Want me to keep looking?"

"If it's not too much trouble, maybe you could widen your search into other states?"

"I reckon. It might take a while seeing as how I'll also being answering and connecting calls."

"Yes. I understand…just whenever you find time to look into it. I'd really appreciate it." At that moment, Tillie desperately wanted to hand Prissy a pound cake, or some other physical expression of her gratitude. Unable to transport baked goods through the telephone, she attempted to satisfy this desire by finding something to compliment Prissy on. Tillie took a chance and said, "And I did want to say…your voice sure sounds clear and strong this morning."

After a pause, Prissy replied, "My granny had a beautiful voice. She was still singing in the choir even up until the Sunday before she died, o' course she was run over by a chicken truck. Anyhow, she always gargled tea made from pine needles, and I do the same. Keeps everything greased and loose."

"Really? That is interesting!"

"Oh, Granny had loads of home cures. She also taught me what to do if I had an earache. She said to break a Betsy Bug in half and squeeze a few drops of its juicy innards inside your ear. Works like a charm."

Once Tillie got the conversation about Appalachian home remedies flowing with Prissy, it became difficult to turn off the tap. She felt guilty about it, but eventually Tillie had to pretend Zeal was calling to her from the other room in order to hang up the phone.

After she had said her final good-byes, Tillie stared at the blank paper in the typewriter in much the same way she had stared at the telephone, as if she could make things happen just by concentrating hard enough.

"Silly woman," she said aloud to herself. "What you need is a bit of nourishment, Chantilly Rose Bransford. That'll get those juices flowing." The mention of juices reminded her of Prissy's earache cure, and Tillie nearly lost her appetite. Regaining her composure, she decided to run home and nibble on the roast chicken she had in the ice box.

Just as she was backing out of her parking spot, Zeal approached her car, waving his arms. She rolled down her window, "Hey there, Pastor. I'm just running home for a bit."

Zeal was panting. "I need to pay a call this evening…" He leaned forward to catch his breath. "To visit a family in the midst of bereavement and strife…" More panting. "I was wondering if I could bring Moses over to your house for you to watch her while I'm gone."

"Well…I suppose so…"

"It won't be more than an hour, I assure you," said Zeal. "I don't feel comfortable leaving her with just anyone. You're the only one I trust."

Tillie knew a flattery with ulterior motives when she heard one, in fact, she had perfected the art, but she found it difficult to say no. In the end, they made arrangements for Zeal to drop by after supper.

374 Verbena Drive

Heidi sat in the kitchen drinking her coffee while Mo ate her hotcakes. "Your Poppy must've gone to McDonald's a hundred times that year you lived with us. He would go and order a couple of those fish sandwiches for you two to have for lunch."

"I remember that," said Heidi. "He would take off the top bun and scrape off the tartar sauce from my sandwich and put it onto his."

"That man did love his condiments." Mo closed the container holding her pancakes and pushed them away from her. "I don't believe I was as hungry as I thought I was."

"You hardly ate any of your hotcakes."

"I reckon they don't taste as good as I remember them." Mo wiped the syrup from her mouth with a paper towel. "Now, have you decided if you're gonna call that Jason fella?"

"Yes. I'm going to do it."

"Alright. Well, I'll give you some privacy. I'm going out to gather some more willow branches." Mo patted Heidi's arm as she walked past her to the back door.

Heidi retrieved the pad of paper from the spare room and brought it to the kitchen. She typed in the digits for Jason's number which she had copied on the paper and listened to her cell phone ring.

"Hello?" said a rough voice.

"Hello…is this Jason?"

"Yes…Heidi?"

"This is Heidi. I—I hope this is a good time."

"Absolutely. I'm so glad you called. You have no idea. Hang on." Heidi could tell that Jason was covering the phone to speak to other people in the room. "Sorry. My sisters' kids are over here. They're good kids, but they're pretty loud."

Heidi struggled to think of what to say next.

"I guess you want to hear about your dad, right?"

"Yes," Heidi answered, relieved that Jason had begun the conversation and got right to the point. "I really know so little about him."

"By the time I got there, Phil had already been in lock up for a few years. He was older than me—I was just a kid, barely legal. He became like a big brother to me. To this day, I don't know why."

"What do you mean?" Heidi asked.

"I was bad news. I had celebrated my 20th birthday by committing first degree armed robbery. It's a miracle I didn't kill anybody. Once I got to prison, I wanted to look tough, but I was actually scared. I think your dad saw right through me, saw how scared I was. I couldn't fool him."

"How long have you been out of prison?"

"Only about six months," Jason answered. "It's been hard, so hard. I'm staying at my mom's, just for a while. I start law school next year, so I'm working a few different jobs right now."

"Law school? That's amazing."

"Yeah. I never would've thought of it back when I was on the outside, but I started reading—the prison library was pretty good, you know, and I realized that I like learning. I also felt like I had to do something with my life, because if I didn't then I would be wasting what your dad did for me."

"Do you mind—I mean, is it okay to talk about what happened the day my dad was—"

"Of course," said Jason. "In some ways it seems like it happened a long time ago, and then there are times when it feels like it was yesterday. I'm okay to talk about it, but I have to start back before the stabbing…if you've got time."

"Yes. I want to know whatever you can tell me."

"Well, me and Phil became friends soon after I got there. He would show me books to read, classic books like *The Hobbit* and

Don Quixote and *The Wizard of Oz* and *Travels with Charley.* He said I needed to fill up my head with good stories of people who've done bad things or had bad things happen to them, but they're brave anyway. The more I read and talked to Phil, the better I felt. He would say, *When you're feeling angry or sad, go find someone you can help. Then you'll feel better.* He liked to quote this one preacher named Charles Spurgeon. If I was feeling like my 10-20 year sentence would last forever, Phil would say, *By perseverance, the snail reached the ark. Don't give up."* Jason chuckled at the memory. "You know, the chaplain brought Phil a book of Spurgeon's sermons. I didn't realize it was with my stack of books until I got out. With all the confidentiality and everything, I wasn't sure how to get it to you, but if you'll give me your address—"

"Yeah. That would be great," Heidi answered.

"Anyway, there was this real bad dude on our block. His name was Anthony. He was huge and mad at everybody, screaming and yelling and making threats. I'm not a very big guy, so I think he picked me out especially to give me a hard time, called me *shrimp* and other things I'm not going to repeat in my Mom's house. Anyhow, when I would get really mad about Anthony, Phil would help me calm down. I was reading *The Odyssey* at the time, so Phil said to imagine that Anthony was Antinous, one of the guys who come around and try to steal Odysseus' wife while he's away. Or Phil said we could call him Cyclops because Anthony had only one good eye. It became a joke for us, something we only talked about when it was just the two of us, until one time when Anthony walked by and I said to Phil real quiet, *Now watch me hit a target that no man has hit before.* It's from the book, when Odysseus is about to shoot an arrow at Antinous. I thought it was funny, you know, no big deal, but Anthony jumped out and went for me. He had a shank hidden in his waistband, a piece of glass with wire wrapped around it and newspaper and duct tape for a handle. Phil saw what was in Anthony's hand, and he stepped right in front of me. It all happened so fast. In just seconds, the guards had Anthony on the floor. I was holding your dad—blood all over his jumpsuit, all over me, too. He was laying on me, and I was yelling and trying to stop the bleeding."

Heidi could tell Jason was fighting to continue talking. His labored breathing sounded like it was coming from a man who had just ran up a steep hill. "You don't have to keep going," she told him.

"No. It's okay. I'm okay." Jason cleared his throat. "I've spent so much time wishing they had gotten him to the infirmary quicker or wondering if the nurses actually tried to save him. I've even wished that I had been the one killed instead of him."

"Don't say that."

"Anyway, you should know that he talked about you all the time, Heidi. He kept your picture right by his bunk. He would tell me how smart you were. He was so proud of you. And you know, it took me a few years, but I finally came up with why those books he picked from the library were his favorites, why he'd go back to them over and over."

"Oh, really? Why's that?" asked Heidi.

"*The Odyssey, The Hobbit*…They were all about going home. That's what he wanted most of all. More than anything else he wanted to come home and see you."

Morgan's Hat, Tennessee, 1941

Just as they had discussed, Zeal arrived at Tillie's home at 6:30 that evening. The shortening of the days as the autumn season plodded on towards winter made it feel later than it actually was, a realization which seemed to confuse and surprise Zeal every fall.

He had never been inside Tillie's house before, though he knew where it was. Zeal was famous for his long walks, so he had passed her house frequently when visiting his flock in their homes. Despite his short stride, he had walked nearly every inch of Morgan's Hat and even outside the city limits, trekking down plenty of the long, county roads deeper in the countryside.

But with Moses in tow and since he didn't own a car, it was fortunate that Tillie lived near the pastorium. A parishioner had lent Zeal an ancient wicker stroller with metal carriage and steel wheels which he had pushed down the street. It was a rickety ride for Moses, but she fell asleep during their stroll, the bumps and wobbles seemed to soothe her, along with the cool autumn breeze.

Zeal parked the stroller by a hedgerow and lifted Moses from her cushion, rearranging the blanket he had wrapped around her. Back at the pastorium, he had prepared a bottle for her in case she got hungry and packed an extra diaper, both of which he tucked next to her, inside her blanket. He cradled the sleeping baby against his chest as he approached the door.

As he was about to knock, Tillie opened the door, anticipating Zeal's arrival. The warm, glowing light from the front room shined behind her curvy silhouette. Soft music played on the radio as the dramatic sound of a trombone swelled in harmony with a swing orchestra.

"Come on in, Pastor," she said.

Zeal froze at the sight of his practical, matronly secretary. Something looked different about her. Was it the apron tied around her waist or the curl of hair which had wriggled free of her pompadour? Or was it seeing Tillie in her own home, at ease in the warm glow of comfort and peacefulness?

He shook himself from his thoughts and entered the house. "I truly appreciate you watching Moses for me. I expect she'll be easy to keep. In fact, she may sleep the entirety of my visit to the Henderson's."

"Oh! With all that's been going on with the baby, I completely forgot about the phone call we got from Nadine Henderson! You were supposed to visit them days ago."

"Not to worry," Zeal said as he laid Moses on Tillie's sofa. "Mrs. Henderson stopped by the pastorium and asked if I could come and talk some sense into her son. He has been drinking away all his earnings, and it's causing quite a bit of grief for his family. As the Good Book says: *For the drunkard shall come to poverty and he shall be clad in rags.*"

Zeal stood awkwardly before leaving. Something made him want to stay.

"What time do they expect you?" Tillie asked, breaking the silence. "You have a bit of a walk ahead of you."

"Yes, I suppose I should get going." He remained standing in the center of the room, listening to the lyrics of the song playing on the radio. The crooner sang of summer skies and birds singing and never-ending love.

"Do you think the music is too loud for Moses? Should I turn down the volume?"

"No," Zeal responded. "It's a lovely song." He sighed deeply. "Goodbye, Mrs. Bransford. I'll hurry back as quick as I can."

As Zeal turned up the collar on his jacket, he shoved his hands in his pockets thinking that the weather had grown chilly. Glancing up at the night sky, he saw no stars. Zeal noticed that leaving the warmth of Tillie's house made the cold air colder and the dark sky darker.

To entertain himself on his walk, he replayed the image of Tillie standing in the doorway. He grasped the small Bible in his jacket pocket and wondered if that beatific glow was what it looked like when the Virgin Mary was visited by the angel Gabriel. Zeal glanced to his right and then to his left to see that he was alone, then he whispered into his upturned collar, "Chantilly." Just the mention of her name warmed his cheeks enough to defend them against the escalating autumn wind.

374 Verbena Drive

After Heidi had given Jason her address in Los Angeles so that he could send her a few things which had belonged to her dad, she thanked him and wished him success in law school. As soon as she hung up, Heidi ran to the spare room, flopped onto the bed, and called Josh to give him an update.

"So how do you feel now that you know more about your Dad?" asked Josh once Heidi had finished recapping her conversation with Jason for him.

"I feel good...and sad. Really sad, but also grateful. Ugh...I sound crazy."

"You don't sound crazy to me. I think we're all capable of feeling more than one thing at the same time, even competing emotions. You're not a robot, Heidi. You're a human being who's dad was killed in prison, and she's just learning about it twenty years later."

"Too bad I'm not a robot. That sounds like your next screenplay—" Heidi changed her voice to sound like a movie preview, "Part human, part machine—a robot with a past discovers what love is when she falls for her toaster, but all she gets in return is burnt toast..."

"*Scorched by Love*. Coming to a theater near you," said Josh. "It really writes itself."

"Let me know when you're ready to start shooting." Heidi chuckled, suddenly feeling lighter than she had in weeks.

"How's your grandma?" Josh asked.

"She's great, such an amazing woman and a born storyteller. You should see these wicker birdhouses she makes." Heidi got off the bed and walked to the bathroom to look out the little window by the sink. She parted the lacy curtain to see Mo standing under the willow tree, tugging at branches. Heidi could just see that Mo's mouth was moving, letting her know that her grandmother was either singing or talking. She liked to think that Mo was giving the willow tree an update about her.

"Maybe I could meet her sometime," Josh said.

"Yes, she would like you. I think I'll try to get back here around Christmas, if it works with my schedule, and maybe you could come with me." Heidi opened the bottom drawer below the bathroom sink again and looked at her dad's old grooming kit and clown-shaped bottle of bubble bath. "And thanks for not asking me when I'm coming home, by the way. I know it must be driving you nuts."

"I'm not pressuring you to do anything. Now, the producers of *Parabola* may be thinking differently…"

"I have to report to the studio on Monday morning, so I'm not in trouble yet." Heidi shut the drawer and opened the one with the medicine bottles. She picked up a bottle and glanced at the label. "Hang on a minute, Josh…" She picked up another bottle and read its label, too. Heidi bent down to look at the collection of the bottles which filled the drawer. "Can I call you back in a little while?" she asked.

"Sure. Is there something wrong?"

"I'm not sure, but I need to talk to Mo."

Heidi hung up her cell phone and went out to the backyard.

"Hey there, Doll Baby." Mo had filled her bucket with hand-picked willow branches and was about to lift it.

"Hey, Mo. Let me help you with that." Without waiting for her to respond, Heidi took the bucket from Mo's hands and carried it to the shed.

"Thanks, honey."

As she set the bucket in the corner of the jam-packed, overcrowded space, Heidi asked, "Are you sick? Those bottles of medicine in the bathroom—I thought they were Poppy's, but they—"

"They're mine, honey." Mo patted Heidi's arm, sympathetically.

"Those are some really powerful pain medications." Heidi scanned her memory from the time since she had first arrived. Mo hadn't seemed sick. In fact, her grandmother had greeted her with an energetic display of bird extermination upon her initial appearance at the front door. But now that she was thinking about it, in the days since she'd been there, Heidi hadn't seen her grandmother eat more than just a few unpopped kernels of popcorn and a bite or two of McDonald's hotcakes. "Are you sick?" she asked again.

Mo sucked her lower lip. Heidi could tell that her grandmother was debating how to respond, how much to reveal. "Yes," she finally said. "I am sick. Doctors told me back in '70 that I had cancer of the ovaries. I was lucky. They found it because I was trying to have another baby. Poppy and I both wanted a big family with lots of kids. Anyhow, I had such a hard time getting pregnant, and if I did, I would lose the baby every time. They ran some tests and found out that I had cancer, so they gave me a hysterectomy."

"Oh, Mo. I'm so sorry."

"I was down for a long while, but so thankful for your daddy. He was four when they took out all my baby-making parts. He was such fun at that age. Do you know that he just loved the Jackson 5? He knew all the words to "ABC" and most of the dance moves." Mo hummed a few bars as she sat on an empty, upturned bucket. "Anyhow, a few years ago, my cancer came back, but this time it's in my bladder and intestines. They tried chemo and radiation. It looked like it was helping at first, but the cancer is still growing. My neighbor Pauline takes me to all my appointments. At my last one, they said I needed something called a urinary diversion. I told them I'd think about it, and on the way home Pauline tried to convince me to have the surgery, but I'm done. I don't want to live out my last days with a bag on the outside of my body holding all my pee. It's fine for some, but it's my choice, and I'm through with all those treatments."

"But if the doctors think it would help…"

"Honey, I love you from here to the hereafter and ten miles past that, but this is one thing you just won't be able to change my mind on. It's made up and that's that."

"But I feel like I've been given a gift one minute, and the next it's being snatched away from me," Heidi lamented.

Mo reached for Heidi's hand and squeezed it. "That makes this time all the sweeter, doesn't it? I can't tell you what your visit has meant to me, Doll Baby. Now, why don't we go on in the house and I'll fix us some lunch. Then you can tell me all about your phone conversation with that Jason fella."

"Okay, Mo. But do you mind if I go for a walk first?" asked Heidi.

"Sure. If you walk the loop of my street, both sides, four times it makes half a mile. Leastwise, that's what Pauline told me. She said she measured it with her car once, which makes no sense at all. Keep in mind, she also plants silk flowers in the beds on either side of her mailbox, so her judgement is a little fishy if you ask me."

"I won't be gone for long. I just want to get a little fresh air."

Heidi walked down Mo's driveway. Her tears were already falling before she had made it to the street.

Morgan's Hat, Tennessee, 1941

Zeal rushed back to Tillie's house as soon as he could tear himself away from the Henderson home. He had duly chastised Willie Henderson for his love of the bottle and prayed over his weaknesses, vowing to return with a handful of deacons if he got word of any more shameful behavior. Nadine, Willie's mother, seemed satisfied with Zeal's intervention.

As Zeal walked down the dark streets, he reflected on the way that Nadine, measuring more than six-feet tall and easily the tallest woman he had ever known, showed genuine love and affection for her towering, thick-headed sons. Zeal determined that they would be lost without their mother.

He thought about his sister Seraphim's suggestion about marrying someone to provide Moses with a mother. Initially, he had shrugged off the notion, claiming that he would be able to raise the baby alone, but now the idea was taking root. Coming home to a hot meal and a happy, loving family sounded like the most perfect situation conceivable, and having Tillie as his wife could be the key ingredient.

As Zeal imagined this very scene, he was on the verge of barging into Tillie's house without knocking first, but stopped himself from committing this crime of poor etiquette. Following his knock, Tillie opened the door for him, a squalling Moses against her chest. "Lands sake! Am I glad to see you! I can't seem to pacify the child!" She transferred the baby to him, nearly throwing Moses into his arms, and went to fetch the bottle. "She guzzled the milk like a hungry fieldhand, but then she started crying and just wouldn't stop! I checked her diaper, and it was dry as a bone. I didn't know what else to do."

Zeal sat down on the sofa, placing Moses in his lap. With his left hand holding her across her chest, he leaned her forward slightly and firmly rubbed her back with his right hand. In a few minutes, Moses let out a substantial belch, followed by a whimper. "She just needed to get rid of a bit of gas," said Zeal as he continued to rub her back. "I've seen her gulp down her milk like she couldn't get enough of it. I think about half of what she gets in her is air."

Tillie frowned. "I haven't had much experience with babies," she explained. "Now I feel as though I've failed the little thing."

"Don't talk that way, Mrs. Bransford! Caring for babies takes some getting used to." With one fluid movement, Zeal settled Moses into her preferred position across his forearm. "You'll get the hang of it."

Tillie stepped into the kitchen without responding. She unscrewed the bottle and rinsed it as she waited for the water to heat up. Zeal followed her, swinging Moses from side to side.

"I don't know that I will get used to it," she finally replied. "I'm just not the mothering type." She stoppered the sink and filled it with soapy water. "It wasn't meant to be."

Zeal watched her, his heart aching in a way he'd never felt before. It wasn't just sympathy or compassion. He was all too familiar with those emotions as he dealt with the troubles of his flock every day. This felt almost like hunger. "What if you had a chance to have a family? Would you take it?"

Tillie turned off the tap but kept her back to Zeal. "What do you mean, Pastor?"

"I mean if there was someone wanting to marry you—someone who would wholly cherish you—and a baby daughter who needed a mother, would you say *yes*?"

Tillie reached for a dishtowel to wipe off her soapy hands and turned around. "When Elmer proposed, I was on Cloud Nine. He was all charm. My daddy approved of him, and my mama thought he was perfect. For our honeymoon, he said we could go to Nashville and stay at the Hermitage Hotel and eat at fancy restaurants.

He made a promise. Instead, he took me to the Kentucky Derby to bet on the horses. No grand hotel or fancy restaurants for me. We ate cold beans from a can. It's not that I minded going without. When he was able to find any jobs, my daddy worked as a locomotive repairman, always had dirt under his fingernails. It wasn't like I was a princess living high up in a castle…I just didn't like being hoodwinked by a liar."

She replaced the towel, then grabbed the ceramic spoon rest which sat by her stovetop, and continued, "I told Elmer how he had lied to me and made me think I couldn't trust him. That was the first time he struck me, but it wasn't the last. The next day, he felt bad about hurting me, so he bought me this." She displayed the spoon rest for Zeal. It was in the shape of a horse's head with a wreath of red roses around its neck. There was a thin crack running down the middle of it.

"Years later, when he was madder than I'd ever seen him, he threw it at me and split open my head…right here." Tillie pointed to the scar that ran along her hairline. "Somehow it broke the spoon rest right in half. I glued it back together, and I keep it sitting by my stove ever since."

"Why did you keep something around that could remind you of such a sad time? Surely you could throw it away and get something else to use instead."

Tillie set the spoon rest back in its usual spot and ran her finger down the crack. "I keep it because it reminds me of how scars heal, but they never disappear. When I look at it, I remember that I am stronger and my head is thicker than what is being thrown my way."

"Well, I would never hurt you," said Zeal in a quiet voice.

"I know, but I can't marry you, Pastor. I closed that book years ago." Tillie unstoppered the sink and let the water swirl down the drain. She rinsed the soap from the bottle and said, "For more than twenty years since he died, I've had my freedom. It's too dear to give it up, even for you and a little baby. To tell the truth, I wonder sometimes if I'm even cut out to be a wife. Did I ever tell you how Elmer died?"

"I don't believe so…no."

"He was sitting down to his supper, complaining about everything

I made and did and said and wore, like usual. My creamed potatoes were too runny, and the fried chicken was burned, and the white beans were too salty, and on and on. Then Elmer picked up a chicken leg and took a big ole bite off it. With his mouth full of food, he was still railing on my cooking, wagging that chicken leg at me, when he started to choke. After a little bit, he couldn't breathe, and his face turned purple. I wacked him on the back a few times, but he just fell over in his chair and died on the kitchen floor. When the doctor came to look at him dead on the floor, he said Elmer probably choked on a chicken bone. But, do you know what? I never cried one tear about him dying. I wouldn't say I was particularly pleased about it, either. I just didn't feel a thing, not a blessed thing."

"You were probably in a state of shock," said Zeal. "And no wonder, being right there when he died."

"I tell you what it was—I was numb. I had taught myself not to feel anything when it came to Elmer, and maybe I also learned to be numb about anything that had to do with marriage or family. It was easier than being sad all the time."

"But all men aren't Elmer Bransford. I wish there was a way I could convince you of my intentions…and of my affection. I've no practice with poetry and such, but I could tell you how I feel. I could tell you that the first time I saw you I thought your hair looked like shiny ripples and waves of sorghum molasses, and that…"

"The best thing you could do for me," Tillie interjected forcefully, breaking off his romantic declarations, "is for us to stay just as we've been. Working at the church and doing good for this town."

"You might grow to love me," Zeal told her. He tried to keep the pleading from his voice.

"I admire you, Pastor, but that's not enough for me to build a marriage on."

"But Moses needs a mother—"

Tillie stopped him. "You're doing a wonderful job caring for her." She smoothed the waves of her hair and adjusted her glasses. "Besides, I haven't given up on finding Miss A, and when I do, Moses *will* have a mother."

374 Verbena Drive

It took her the entire length of one side of Verbena Drive for Heidi to stop crying. On her walk, she reflected on the massive, hulking load of news she'd received in the space of just a few hours which was bearing down on her like she was carrying a backpack full of bricks. Talking to Jason, a man who had been with her father in his last moments before he had died in prison, and hearing that her grandmother was diagnosed with a late-stage, invasive cancer had given her a desire to hit the streets. Similarly, before she had made her impulsive cross country drive to see Mo, she had also felt a weight. But back in L.A. she couldn't pinpoint the location of the agonizing heaviness or what was causing it. Now she was aching in such a profound and painful way, and again she was compelled to move. Only this time, she was content just to walk, instead of renting a car, driving day after day without telling anyone where she was going.

She wasn't paying much attention to the houses on the street until she passed a brick house with orange, yellow, and rust-colored artificial flowers planted at the base of the mailbox. It was right across from Mo's house, so Heidi assumed it must be where Pauline lived.

A middle aged woman with a cheetah print sweatshirt and bubblegum pink leggings walked around from the back of the house. She was half wresting/half carrying a life-sized scarecrow which she eventually sat on a rocking chair on her front porch.

"Hey!" the woman called when she saw Heidi. She was waving her arms, her bracelets making a clacking sound as they knocked together. "You must be Heidi!" The woman hurried over to where Heidi was standing on the street. "I'm Pauline, a friend of your granny."

"Hey, Pauline. It's nice to meet you."

"Oh, sweetie, I'm so glad you're here! It's just what your granny needed, to see some of her kinfolk."

"I can't thank you enough for taking care of Mo while she's been sick. I had no idea."

Pauline put her hands on her hips and shook her head. "You know how these elderly folks can be—they either tell you about every little ache and pain or they don't tell you nothing. I believe your granny don't want to be a burden, so she mostly keeps it to herself, but Mrs. Seek has always been so sweet to me. I love her like she's my own Mama."

"She told me that you tried to convince her have the surgery. I wish she'd change her mind," Heidi said sadly.

"Her body's been through a lot, hon. I know how you feel, but I reckon she should get to say when she's had enough."

"I haven't had a chance to do any research about her diagnosis. Mo said you go to her appointments with her. Do you know what to expect? Like how long people with her condition generally live?"

"It's hard to say, but I would guess some kind of infection will eventually take her. Until then, your granny is appreciating every day like it's her last…in her own way, of course. If it was me, I would probably want to use my last months on Earth doing crazy stuff, like going to Vegas or jumping out of an airplane or something, but she mostly just stays around the house. She likes me to take her to the cemetery every so often to look at Mr. Jimbo's grave and your daddy's, too. I think it gives her some comfort to see where her body will lie once it's all over."

Heidi wasn't accustomed to hearing people talk so candidly about death. It was a shock, and she felt anger rising inside her. It seemed that Pauline had also accepted Mo's death without a fight. What if something could be done? Experimental treatments or wholistic medicine? Heidi wanted to say all of this, but she suddenly felt too tired to sort out the words.

"So…when are you going back to California?" Pauline asked. "I've never been farther west than Missouri myself."

"I'll leave tomorrow or maybe Saturday. It all depends on when I can get a flight out." Heidi felt sick at the thought of leaving her grandmother alone.

"Hon, would it make you feel better if I give you my cell number? I check in on your granny at least twice a day. You can call me if you're ever worried, and if anything changes, I can give you a call."

"That would be great! Thank you so much."

"Let me run in the house and grab a piece of paper and a pen." Pauline hustled to her front door, stopping to rearrange the slumping scarecrow. Before going inside, she called over her shoulder, "And if you've got the number for any of them good-looking, hunky fellas from those Hallmark movies, you can write them down for me!"

Morgan's Hat, Tennessee, 1941

On Tuesday, Tillie was grateful that Zeal was staying home to care for Moses instead of coming in to the office. She couldn't bear to see his hang-dog expression, the one he had worn when he had left her house the night before. He hadn't pleaded outright, but his face had been pitiable. If he had had his shoes off and she had seen the disgraceful state of his socks again, she might've married him right then and there in a moment of weakness. It was the same when she had been a girl, and she had wanted to take in every stray dog and cat which dragged itself near their little shotgun house. Tillie felt sure that refusing Zeal had been the right choice, but it still pained her to see anyone miserable, especially if it was in her power to alleviate that misery.

As she sat down at her desk, she saw the blank sheet of paper, still threaded in her typewriter, waiting for her to write Zeal's sermon. She told herself to get busy writing. This was a way to make Pastor Cooley feel better, to take things off his plate, such as preparing his sermons. They could conceivably go on in this way for years—her seeing to various tasks, both significant and insignificant, and him shepherding his flock. Perhaps the embarrassment related to his proposal would fade away with time, and things would return to normal with no more foolish talk of love and marriage.

Just as Tillie was about to begin typing, she heard a voice coming from the sanctuary. "Mrs. Bransford...yoo-hoo!"

A young woman entered the office carrying a basket full of various,

wrapped packages. She had bright red-orange hair and round, freck-led cheeks. Tillie recognized her at once.

"Why, Adell Padgett! Your mother and I were just talking about you yesterday, but she didn't mention that you were in town."

"My aunt carried me home last night. She needed to see to a few things in Nashville, and I was keen to see Mother, so she dropped me off to spend a few days in Morgan's Hat. Of course, I should've guessed Mother'd have me running errands the minute I set a toe inside the store." Adell set a small package on Tillie's desk. "She asked me to bring you this can of baby powder."

"How thoughtful! How have you been, dear? Do you like Kentucky?" Tillie asked, looking intently at the girl. She wondered how she would know if Adell had given birth in the last few months. It was obvious she had blossomed into womanhood in all the apparent ways, but beyond that Tillie was unsure what signs she should be looking for.

"Oh, I'm fine. Glad as anything to be home, if I can say as much without sounding ungrateful. Aunt Marigold is kind, but she sure is strict."

"Is that right?"

"Yes, indeed, Mrs. Bransford! I never get to meet any fellas at all. I suppose Mother and Daddy asked her to keep me respectable, but I wonder if they asked her to keep me under lock and key! 'Cuz that's just about what she does!"

"I'm sure she's just trying to be a good aunt to you."

"I know, but Auntie never had children of her own to bring up, so she likes to think the worst of anyone on the young side of thirty, and I get the dirty end of that deal! I mean, what do you think—a girl of seventeen who's never been kissed? I'm ashamed of it! I've never even been close to it!"

"So you've never had a fella?" asked Tillie as she examined Adell's face for any sign of dishonesty or depravity. "Not even a handsome beau to sit next to on a hayride or at a church picnic?

Adell sighed dramatically. "I'm afraid not. I must give off some kind of odor that makes fellas steer clear of me."

Satisfied with her candidness, Tillie decided she didn't need to interrogate Adell further. They said good-bye, and she returned

her attention to the blank typing paper which was waiting to hold
Zeal's words for Sunday.

She had no idea what the topic for the sermon should be, so
she decided to just start typing. "Good morning and welcome to
the Lord's House at Berea Baptist church," Tillie read aloud as she
pressed the keys, hoping that her brain would take off from there.
Instead, she was motionless. Her mind drew a blank.

Suddenly, the telephone rang causing her to jump and knock over
her purple handbag which she had left sitting on the desk instead
of putting it the lower drawer as she usually did.

"Hello?" she said as soon as she had removed her earring and
picked up the receiver.

"This is Prissy from the switchboard."

"Yes! Good morning, Prissy! It's good to hear your voice." Tillie
attempted to keep the phone to her ear as she reached towards the
floor to pick up the scattered contents of her purse.

"You had asked for a list of music schools in and around our area.
I wrote them all out, and I wanted to see if you'd like to come by
and pick up the list."

"Why, that is so considerate of you! Would noon be a good time
to stop by?"

"Yes, ma'am. I'll be here…oh, and I took the liberty of brewing
up some of the tea I told you about."

"Prissy, you are such a dear! I will see you soon!"

Tillie returned the phone to its cradle and finished cleaning up
her belongings. The recipe box, which she had never removed from
her purse, had opened and the cards had flown in every direction.
She got on her hands and knees, picking them up and stacking them.
One had scooted under her desk. As she reached to grab the card
with its recipe for Lola Tharpe's Lemon Cheese Cake, she noticed
for the first time that there was writing on the back, words scribbled
in the distinct scrawl of an elderly hand. It said:

Cincinnati Conservatory of Music
Highland Avenue and Oak Street
Cincinnati, Ohio

Above the address, two words were written in clear block letters:

Alice Mead. It seemed that Tillie had been carrying around the name she was looking for ever since Mrs. Gautreaux had given her the recipe box. She just hadn't thought to turn the cards over and look at the back of them.

She envisioned Willadeene Lathrop looking for any piece of paper within reach on which to jot the young woman's address. Perhaps she had just made the Lemon Cheese Cake, or maybe it was Alice's favorite dessert. Whatever the circumstances, Tillie felt confident that this woman was Moses' mother, and she had to find her. Together with the tingling sensation she felt along her forearms and across the tops of her ears, all of her church secretary powers of intuition were indicating that this was it.

Not wanting to wait until noon to pick up the list of music schools, Tillie grabbed her purse. She decided to go right away, and if the music school in Cincinnati wasn't on the list, she'd find that, too.

As she backed out of her parking spot, Tillie didn't notice Zeal standing in the shadow of the doorway of his house, watching her drive away. As soon as she was gone, he bundled Moses in a blanket and carried her to the church.

"We'll just pop in for a moment to get a book," he said to the baby. "It's an autobiography of Charles Spurgeon, a famous English preacher. It's time we begin your theological education, Moses, and I think you'll find Spurgeon's thoughts especially interesting."

Zeal switched on the desk lamp and quickly found the book. Then he turned to leave. He stopped to look at Tillie's desk, sighing forlornly at her cushions and knickknacks, and spotted something on the floor by the filing cabinet. It glittered as it caught the sunlight coming in from the window. He tucked the book under his arm, stepped around the desk and picked up the object, instantly recognizing it to be one of the earrings Tillie often wore. It was made from purple jewels fashioned together to resemble a cluster of grapes. He began to set it on her desk by the telephone, but changed his mind. Instead, he slipped the earring inside the pocket of his cardigan.

As he stepped into the sanctuary, the stolen earring burning in his pocket, Zeal whispered, "Forgive me, Lord. I am a weak and sinful man."

374 Verbena Drive

When Heidi came back inside Mo's house, she found her grandmother humming as she cooked ground beef in a cast iron skillet.

"What are you making, Mo?" asked Heidi.

"Oh, it's something I grew up eating, and I suddenly had a hankering for. It's called Railroad Pie, though I'm not sure how it got that name. It's just hamburger meat, tomato soup, chopped-up onion, can of creamed corn, and some spices in a skillet. Then you top it with cornbread batter and bake it."

"It seems like a good sign that you have an appetite," Heidi said, hopefully.

"Ah, it comes and goes. Sometimes I go to a lot of trouble to fix something up, and then I can't eat a bite of it."

Heidi stared at Mo's curved back for a moment before saying, "I've got to go check on something. I'll be right back."

Heidi went in the spare room and turned on her laptop. She searched for non-stop flights home and found one leaving first thing in the morning. She could drop off her rental car at the airport, wheels up at 7:15 a.m. and be in LAX before 10:00 a.m., California time. She felt conflicted about leaving, but she knew she had to get back. Before booking the flight, she called Josh again.

"So here's what's going on," she said to him after he had answered, skipping over the customary *hellos* and *how are you*. "My grandmother is sick. She has cancer. She didn't want to tell me, but I found her stash of oxycodone while I was snooping around the bathroom. I also found a flight leaving in the morning, but I feel like I'm abandoning her. What should I do?"

"Wow! I'm so sorry, Heidi. I don't know what to tell you, but I think you're discussing it with the wrong person. Go and ask your grandma what she wants you to do."

"I know what she'll say. She's the most unselfish person in the world. She'll tell me to go."

"Or if she asks you to stay longer, you'll know that she really needs you."

"She'd never ask me to change my plans," Heidi replied confidently. "It goes against her nature. Being here with her, it feels like Mo is the first person who's ever been okay with me just being me. She's not asking anything from me—to be someone or something other than my real self. No agenda. No plans. Just me."

"So, do I go into that category, too? Do you think I ask too much?" asked Josh. Heidi could hear the hurt in his voice. She paused to carefully consider her response.

"It's not that you ask too much. I should be able to deal with people asking things from me. I mean, I can accept being obligated to others, like you and my mom and my job. My time here just feels like a vacation, like a break from high expectations. Please, don't be mad, Josh."

"I'm not mad." Josh forced a long breath out his nose, allowing Heidi to hear his signature nose whistle. "Just go and talk to your grandma before you book anything. The situation stinks, but I bet you can find ways to make it better—better for her and for you."

"Okay. I love you."

"Love you, too," said Josh. "Let me know what you decide."

Mo was sitting at the dining room table when Heidi walked back in the kitchen.

"Railroad Pie is in the oven." Mo looked down at the wind-up egg timer in her hand. "Still has twenty minutes to go. Do you need something else to eat while we wait? I've got some boiled eggs and some jello salad…" She began to get up from her chair, but Heidi stopped her.

"I can wait for the Railroad Pie. It smells great." Heidi opened the refrigerator. "How about I pour us both a glass of tea?"

Mo smiled. "That would hit the spot, Doll Baby. Thank you."

Heidi took down two glasses from the cabinet, added ice, and poured tea from the pitcher Mo kept in the refrigerator. After taking a big gulp, Mo traced her finger along the grapevine cut into the outside of the glass. "I always loved these glasses. I s'pose they'll be yours when I'm gone, along with everything else in the house."

Heidi wanted to argue with Mo and ask her to stop talking about her cancer, but she just stared at her glass of tea. "I was looking at flights…" Heidi began, but her voice trailed off.

"Did you find one that'll work out for you?" asked Mo. "Sounds like you need to get started on that math teacher movie. From what I see on TV these days, we could all use something decent to watch for a change."

"I did find a flight, but I feel so bad leaving you." Heidi's lip trembled, then she broke down and sobbed, dropping her head onto her arms where they rested on the table.

"Oh, honey! You poor thing!" Mo grabbed a tissue from the box on the table and gave it to her. "I wish you hadn't found my medicine, but I s'pose it's for the best. We need to get a few things out in the open, so we can talk it through, alright?" Heidi nodded her head, but didn't say anything. "I don't want you worrying about me. I've got doctors and nurses a-plenty, and Pauline is awful good to me. I can still get around and do what needs doing. One of the deacons and his wife pick me up every Sunday for church, and I've got my special project out in the shed. You need to go and make your movie and marry your fella, if you decide to. If I kept you from doing any of that, it would hurt me more than any operation those surgeons want to give me."

"But how can I not worry about you? You'll be 2,000 miles away."

"We can talk on the phone every day, if you like. And you can come back and visit anytime." Mo stood up and opened a kitchen drawer. She rummaged around for a minute and brought out a key attached to a keychain with a cut-out of Elvis Presley, hip cocked and microphone in hand. "Here's a housekey for you," she said. "It's yours to use whenever you want. You don't even have to call first."

Heidi sat up and blew her nose in the tissue. "Christmas is just a few months away. I could come back to see you then."

Mo grabbed Heidi's chin in her wrinkled hand. "Nothing would make me happier, Doll Baby. You come and see me and bring your fella. I'll make ambrosia and divinity and peanut butter balls, and we'll watch old Christmas movies."

"Okay." Heidi took a shaky breath. "And I will call you every day until then."

"That would be so nice, honey." Mo kissed Heidi's forehead. "It's gonna be okay."

Heidi went back into the spare room and booked her flight home. When she re-emerged into the kitchen, she returned with a plan. "All set," she announced, trying to sound cheerful.

"Perfect timing," said Mo. "Lunch is all ready."

They sat down to eat, and Heidi made a suggestion. "If you feel like it, would you like me to take you to the cemetery after lunch? It feels great outside, and I would like to see Daddy and Poppy's graves before I fly back to L.A."

"That's a wonderful idea, Doll Baby. I'd love that."

After lunch, they cleaned up the dishes and drove outside the city limits to a sprawling cemetery. All through the half-hour drive, the afternoon sun had streamed through the car windows, and now that they had parked the car and were walking to the family plots, Heidi still felt its reassuring warmth, as if the sun chose to shine on them in particular.

On the way to the cemetery, they had stopped at a plant nursery and picked up two hostas. Mo had said that, as a rule, Jimbo didn't approve of overly showy flowers, so the leafy green plants would be ideal decorations for the graves.

Heidi carried the plants as she followed Mo to the plots. Mo opened her purse and pulled out a bundle wrapped in a striped dish towel. As she unwrapped the bundle revealing a small garden spade, Mo swiveled her head to look around them. "You keep an eye out while I dig a couple of holes, honey," she told Heidi.

"Are we not supposed to do this? I don't want to get in any trouble."

"It's not against the law or anything. The caretaker just doesn't like people doing their own gardening at the cemetery." Mo got down on her knees, wiping off Jimbo's headstone with the dish towel, then she began digging. "I'd be fine with that except they don't give families much to look at around here. It's mowed regularly and there's no weeds, but it makes me sad when nothing but grass is growing. I prefer a little variety."

Heidi looked at the nearby graves. She saw little, faded American flags and wreaths made from artificial flowers and a teddy bear with matted fur and a tattered blue ribbon around its neck. "And I guess you wouldn't want to set out fake flowers?" she posed the idea tentatively.

"Certainly not. When something that's not meant to be outdoors is left outdoors for a long time with rain and sun pouring down on it…well, it gets to looking forgotten." Mo had finished the first hole, so she gestured for Heidi to hand her one of the plants. She carefully slid the hosta from its plastic pot and placed it in the hole. Heidi watched the movements of Mo's age-worn hands as she lovingly patted the dirt around the base.

"I'll dig the other hole," said Heidi, and Mo handed the spade to her.

"I like to plant it just where their heads would be. It's a pleasant notion to think of them looking up and seeing something pretty growing just above them." Mo removed a jar from her purse and carefully unscrewed the lid. Though it had once held mayonnaise, she had filled the cleaned, empty jar with water before they left. Now she poured half of its contents on the newly-planted Hosta. "Of course, I know that it's silly to think of them looking at anything now or to even tell myself that Phillip and Jimbo are down there. But sometimes we have to do silly things so that we can keep on living and doing what needs to be done, especially when what's happened to us just doesn't make sense."

"Is it hard for you to keep going?" Heidi asked as she placed the second hosta in the hole she had dug.

"Sometimes," Mo answered. "Things don't always turn out the way we want them to, so you have to have something that stays the same and props you up when you feel like you might take a tumble. It's like how deep we made these holes. For a plant to survive being put in the ground, the hole has to be pretty deep. If

it isn't, the roots will suffocate, and without good roots, the plant will starve to death."

Mo gave Heidi the dish towel so that she could wipe off her hands. She thought about her grandmother's wise words, how she should look for things in her own life which would keep her grounded. She felt like she'd mostly lived a shallow life, but maybe that was because she was trying to walk inside her skin without really knowing much about herself or her history. It was like she was trying to drive a race-car with only one wheel, staggering and weaving precariously, instead of assertively meeting the road on a full set of dependable tires.

Heidi helped Mo stand up, and they both brushed the dirt from their clothes.

"Do you think the caretaker will let you keep the plants in the ground or will he dig them up and toss them?" Heidi asked.

"Hard to say," Mo said as she rewrapped the spade with the dirty dish towel before putting both back in her purse. "But one thing we can say—we made this little spot a tiny bit prettier today." She squeezed Heidi's arm. "That'll help me sleep better tonight."

Morgan's Hat, Tennessee, 1941

Tillie drove to Prissy's house located one street over from the busy town square. The switchboard was operated in the house, and each of the previous owners had been telephone operators, too. She knocked on the door and waited to hear Prissy call out, "Come on in," before letting herself inside. Prissy was so accustomed to wearing the headphones which remained attached to the switchboard wall unit, it was as if she was also irreversibly wired to it.

"I laid the list on the table by the door," said Prissy. "And there's a jar of tea next to it."

Tillie picked up both the paper and the jar and stepped over to Prissy at her post. "I am ever so grateful for your help," said Tillie, scanning the list of music schools.

"Do you know which one you want to call?" Prissy asked as she took a jack from one hole and placed it in a hole next to a light. Then she asked the caller a few questions and moved the jack to a different spot.

"I sure do," Tillie replied once Prissy had completed the call. "The Cincinnati Conservatory of Music. Right here." She pointed to the paper.

"You head on back to the church, and I'll put the long distance call through to you there."

"You are a wonder, Prissy! I've never seen anyone manage so many tasks at the same time!"

"I watched my mama do the same job when I was a baby, and then took over for her when her bursitis gave her too much trouble. It's like most things—becomes second nature once you get the hang of it, like riding a bicycle or buck dancing. Take my Uncle Shorpy. He could juggle one-handed on account of him losing his arm when he was a boy and working as a greaser in a coal mine in Alabama. Got run over by a coal car and chopped his arm clean off. Anyhow, Shorpy could get four apples going at the same time, all of 'em up in the air, and then he'd take a bite out of one of 'em. I remember one time…"

"Well, I am truly impressed!" Tillie interrupted. "I better let you get back to your switchboard."

"Oh, before you go—" Prissy began but was interrupted by another call. Once she was finished, she asked, "Did you know you're missing an earring?"

Tillie placed her hands on her ears. "Oh dear! Isn't that a shame! And these are my favorite earbobs." She unfastened her lone earring and dropped it in her purse, then began backing out of Prissy's house before she could start talking again.

As she drove to the church, Tillie pondered this newfound perspective concerning Prissy's personality. She never would've suspected the taciturn switchboard operator to be quite so chatty. Perhaps people were more complex than she often assumed. Sometimes the surface needed a little scratching to see what was underneath. She was determined to bring up this epiphany at the next meeting of the Davis County League of Church Secretaries to hear their thoughts on the subject, especially in relation to church matters. Once she had arrived at the office, Tillie took a minute to look for her earring, but gave up when the phone rang.

"Hello…this is Tillie Bransford," she responded, excitedly. After identifying herself, she made inquiries to the school receptionist about a former student. "Her name is Alice Mead. I'm not sure how long ago she was there."

"Ah, yes. Miss Mead is a talented violinist." Tillie heard the sound of a drawer opening and closing. "It is very rare for a woman to join an orchestra, though we hope that will change over time. We like to keep in contact with all our students after they graduate and go out into the world to make their mark. It's a point of pride for the conservatory." The woman paused, and Tillie listened to her shuffle papers. The receptionist gave Tillie details about Alice's most recent job and suggested that she contact the orchestra.

It was dark outside by the time Tillie had the telephone number for the hotel where Alice was staying, and gathering all of the information would've been impossible without Prissy's help. The manager of the hotel had explained that Alice was out of her room presently, but he would be happy to leave a message for her. Tillie considered the idea, but decided Alice might not return her call. She didn't want to scare her or make Alice think she was in trouble. Instead, Tillie asked when the members of the orchestra would be back in their rooms. The manager recommended that she telephone mid-morning the next day.

On the paper where she was had made numerous notes throughout the day, she wrote a final reminder:

Buy prissy a teapot.

She thought a small gift to show her appreciation to the switchboard operator would be a nice gesture.

As she prepared to leave for the day, Tillie saw a strip of light under the door to Zeal's private office. She opened the door and stepped inside, seeing that the desk lamp was switched on. "That's odd," she said aloud to herself.

Looking at his desk chair, she was surprised to realize that she wished Zeal were sitting there, so she could tell him about her day. Then Tillie amended that notion. She wasn't ready to tell him about Alice yet, not until she could give him concrete and verified information about Moses' mother. But if everything went well, Alice would be reunited with her daughter, arrangements would be made, and Zeal would understand that he had only made his proposal of marriage because he had wanted Tillie to help him raise the child. He would miss Moses, but things would fall back into place, right where they belonged. "It's for the best," she said to the empty chair. "You'll see."

Agreeing with her own interpretation of the situation, Tillie switched off the lamp and went home.

374 Verbena Drive

"How's the weather in California?" Mo asked. She was sitting in her favorite recliner with her feet up, the television on but muted.

"Warm and sunny," Heidi responded. This was the regular preamble to their calls in the routine they had established in the month since Heidi had left. Mo always started off by asking about the weather, and Heidi nearly always responded, "Warm and sunny."

They had found that the best time for them to chat was before Heidi headed to the studio each morning. By then, Mo had already been up and going for a couple of hours, so she was ready for a snack and a break to watch her favorite show, *Murder, She Wrote*.

"Well, it's raining cats and dogs here, a real frog-wash. The leaves on the driveway are as slick as anything. Getting the mail yesterday, I nearly slipped. Thing is I was just wearing this flimsy, old housecoat so I would've showed all my neighbors my underpants."

"Why don't you let Pauline get your mail? We don't need you falling and breaking a hip," Heidi scolded.

"You sound just like her. Pauline was ready to tan my hide. She came running out of her house—I guess she was watching me from her front window—silly, snooping thing should work for the CIA—and she grabbed ahold of me and carted me back to the house."

"I'm glad you're okay," said Heidi. "Speaking of mail, I got a package from Jason yesterday," said Heidi.

"The fella who was in prison with your daddy?"

"That's right. He sent a book of sermons by Charles Spurgeon.

From what Jason told me, it was one of Daddy's favorites. Inside the book, I found a picture I drew for him when I was little—which I have absolutely no memory of making—and a photograph of me. It looks like it's a school picture. There's one of those fake library backdrops behind me."

"I remember sending that to him. Warms my heart to know you have 'em now."

"Inside the book, there's some writing on the front flap," Heidi went on. "It says, 'I would go to the deeps a hundred times to cheer a downcast spirit. It is good for me to have been afflicted…'"

Mo recited the rest of the quote along with Heidi: "'…that I might know how to speak a word in season to one that is weary.'"

"You know the quote?" asked Heidi.

"I sure do. It's from Mr. Spurgeon. And such a good way to think about how to act when you're troubled. I always used to tell your daddy that he should find someone to help when he's feeling down."

"He must've been listening to you, because he gave Jason the same advice. I'll take a picture of what he sent me and text it to you, so you can see it."

"This phone is a marvel," Mo responded. "To think I could get pictures on a telephone. I appreciate you buying it for me, though I know the bill must be sinfully high."

"I was happy to do it. It was nice of Pauline to come over and get it set up for you."

"She's good at all that sort of thing. She's been a Mary Kay lady for years, so she had to figure out how to reach her customers and such. She tried to give me a makeover a few years ago but I told her it'd be cheaper and more efficient for me to just put a grocery bag over my head than to go to all the trouble and expense of buying a mess of that makeup."

"Oh, Mo! You should've let her do it!" Heidi exclaimed.

"Well, maybe I will. She's a fairly persistent saleslady."

"Did you ever sell anything like that?"

"Makeup? Certainly not. I never had the face for that kind of work. In fact, I never sold anything at all. I was better at working where nobody could see my face, like when I worked the switchboard in our little town for a couple of years after I turned sixteen."

"What was that like?" Heidi asked.

"It was a fine job, paid pretty well but the hours could get tedious. The switchboard was in the home of a family in town. At the time, all the houses were on a ten-party line, meaning that when a call was made, it rang in all ten houses. Every house had their own ring—two shorts and a long or three shorts, something like that. Everybody just memorized their own ring and learned to sleep through the rings that they weren't s'posed to answer. Even the dogs learned to ignore the other rings."

"Sounds like a complicated job," said Heidi.

"It could be. Calls had to be answered all the time, night and day. I mostly did the regular hours shift—breakfast to supper—but there were a few times when I had to run the switchboard overnight. There was one time when a call came through about a house on fire. I had to go outside and around to the back of the house to pull the alarm for the fire department. Soon as I did, the switchboard lit up like a Christmas tree with people just wanting to know what was on fire. I started answering, '32 Maple Street' without even asking where they wanted to connect to. Then one fella said, 'Hold your horses, I need to make a call.' We got to talking and before you know it, that fella asked me if I wanted to go to Sullivan's Drug Store for a Coca-Cola."

"Did you go with him?"

"I sure did. And a year later, we were married!"

"That was Poppy? What a great story, Mo. You really need to write this stuff down."

"I don't s'pose anybody else would think my life was all that interesting."

"Well, I would definitely like to have a copy of your stories."

"How's this…I have a few birdhouses under construction right now. As soon as I get them done, I'll start writing down some of my memories. Would that suit you?"

"Yes, ma'am!" Heidi responded, enthusiastically.

"It's starting to get too cool to be outside much anyhow—leastwise for those of us who don't live in California."

"I better get going, Mo. I'll talk to you tomorrow. Love you!"

"I love you from here to the hereafter and ten miles past that, honey!"

Mo sat her cell phone on the table by her recliner and turned up the volume on her television show. "Let's see what old Jessica Fletcher is up to today," she said as she settled into her recliner.

Morgan's Hat, Tennessee, 1941

On Wednesday morning, Tillie arranged with Prissy to put in a call at precisely 10:30 a.m. at the hotel where Alice's orchestra was staying. In the hour and half while she waited, Tillie looked for things to clean. She swept the foyer and wiped down the front windows. She considered finding a ladder to clean the tall, arched windows in the sanctuary, but decided she wasn't dressed for that type of work.

She glanced at the clock on her desk and saw that it was only 9:30—an hour to go. Though decades earlier she had vowed never to clean Zeal's office, she was desperate for something to keep her busy.

The day that he had found Moses on the doorstep, Zeal had begun to tidy his office, but he hadn't gotten very far. Much of the trash had been cleared away, but there were still books stacked on the floor in teetering columns, precariously assembled so that they often came crashing down at the slightest provocation. Entering the room and seeing what looked like ancient ruins, but just on a smaller scale than the Colosseum, Tillie was even afraid to sneeze. On top of some of these stacks, were dirty coffee cups or saucers displaying only a crust of bread and a smear of red jelly. Tillie gathered the dishes in a box she found in the broom closet, then she began re-shelving the books.

In terms of Zeal's extensive library, the bare bones of the organizational system Tillie had created when she first came to work at Berea Baptist was still in place, so she mainly had to place the wayward books lying on the floor in the empty spaces along the shelves. Before long, she was able to see both the floor and the top of Zeal's desk. She clucked disapprovingly when she saw the ink blotter calendar with the year **1920** written at the top and the name of the bank where she had opened her first bank account: the **H. H. Jarvis Federal Savings & Loan**. More than twenty years had passed since she had given it to Zeal, and it was still there.

Tillie spied something tucked beneath the calendar. It was sticking out just under the lower, right corner. Sitting in Zeal's chair, she slowly pulled it out with her finger and saw that it was a square of thick, cream-colored cotton paper. In the center of the square was a photograph of a young girl with billows of jet black hair on top of her head and bewitchingly dark eyes. Her skin was pale, and she wore a lacy collar and a short string of pearls. The picture faded below her collar, and Tillie could just make out the tops of the puffed fabric resting on the woman's shoulders. "Lovely," Tillie breathed. At the bottom of the photograph, someone had written: *Olivia 1902*.

As she was examining the photograph, the phone began to ring. Tillie hustled to her desk and answered, "Hello!"

"Here's the number you asked for," said Prissy.

Tillie heard a click, and then she was connected to the hotel manager.

"Andrew Jackson Hotel…Mr. Bishop speaking."

"Good morning," said Tillie. "Could you please connect me to Miss Alice Mead's room?"

"Of course. Please hold the line…"

While she waited, Tillie popped a piece of hard candy in her mouth. The phone rang twice, then a woman answered, "Hello?"

To stop the telephone receiver from shaking, Tillie had to hold it with both hands. She closed her eyes, then said, "Miss Mead?"

"Yes."

"My name is Chantilly Bransford, and I am the secretary at Berea Baptist church—"

"Oh!"

"Please! Don't hang up!" Tillie nearly sprang out of her chair.

"What do you want?" Alice asked.

"I think you know why I'm calling."

"It's about—about the baby. Has something happened? Is she alright?"

"Oh yes!" Tillie assured her. "She's as right as rain and has the sweetest disposition."

"That's a relief."

"I wanted to find you, because…" Tillie chose her words carefully. "Because I believe you must miss the child powerfully and we—Pastor Cooley and I—wanted you to know that leaving her here at the church doesn't have to be the final word on the matter."

"You don't understand," Alice replied. "There's no other way."

"There's always another way."

"Not this time. You see, both of my parents are gone. My mother died just after I was born, and my father died when I still very young. I was bundled off to one elderly aunt after another, and now they're all gone, too."

"And the baby's father?"

"We weren't married, and he wants nothing to do with me or the baby." Alice's voice caught in her throat. Tillie could tell she was trying not to cry. "You can't imagine what it feels like to be deceived by the man who said he loved you."

"Trust me, I can imagine that very clearly, Miss Mead."

"I've had to put all of it behind me and concentrate on my music. I've made my peace with this situation. I'm learning to be content with being alone."

"But don't you see? You're not alone. You have a baby, and if you come back to Morgan's Hat, we will help you."

"But how can I face you when you know what I did? I could just die of shame. You must think I'm an awful person."

"It's not my job to think what kind of person anyone is. It's my job to help." Tillie held her breath and prayed silently.

"You want me to come to Morgan's Hat?" asked Alice.

"Yes. Please come and see your baby and listen to Pastor Cooley's counsel. You may change your mind. But if you're still set on leaving her, well…mothers often have to give up their children, but it's important that we handle the details in a proper way. We will help you sort out what's best for you and Baby Moses."

"Baby Moses?"

"Ah, well—Pastor hated to just call her 'the baby,' so he gave her a name. He took it from the Bible, seeing that Moses was lifted from the basket floating amongst the reeds of the Nile, and your baby was lifted from a fruit crate with a picture of the Nile on its label. Pastor Cooley is a great expert of the Holy Scriptures." Tillie waited to hear her response to the name, but Alice was silent. "Nothing is official. I'm sure it can be changed—"

"I like the name. I hadn't given her one. I just couldn't bear to name her when she was born. I was afraid of getting attached."

"But I gather you got attached anyhow?"

Alice sighed. "It was hard not to. She was so tiny and helpless. But I had made a plan, and I was determined to stick to it. I knew I would give her up, so I set the crate on the step and went to hide in the bushes. I stayed out in the woods until I saw Pastor Cooley fetch her. You have to believe me—I kept watching until I knew she was safe."

"I'm sure you did, dear, which shows me that you love her, but it's not too late to make this right. Please, come and see us."

"I do have a free day tomorrow. I would have to check the bus schedule…"

"I'll be here all day. Come directly to the church, and then I'll take you over to your baby."

"I don't know why I'm letting you talk me into this."

"Because I think that deep down, you want to see your daughter."

Mo was in her bedroom, dusting the top of her bureau, when her cell phone rang. She pulled it out of the pocket of her floral housecoat. "Hello? That you, Heidi?"

"Yes, ma'am. Happy Thanksgiving!"

"Happy Turkey Day to you, too, honey. How's the weather in California?

"Warm and sunny. How's it there?"

"Pretty chilly and cloudy today. You gonna have any turkey?" Mo asked. "Or do they even eat turkey and stuffing in Hollywood?"

"I'm going over to Josh's apartment. He's fixing supper for us—turkey, dressing, rolls—everything."

"He can cook, too? Honey, you got to marry that fella for sure!" Mo picked up a framed photograph from her bureau and wiped it with a rag. "Thank you for sending me this picture of you. It's just beautiful."

"Oh, you're welcome. I was wearing the clip-on earrings you gave me that day, so I asked a friend to take a picture of me. You said you liked looking at the earrings instead of wearing them…"

"And I've been looking at them every day—such a blessing. I have a few other things set aside to give you, too."

"Are you excited about Christmas? I can't wait to come out and see you."

"I sure am! I love celebrations." Feeling a little winded, Mo tucked the rag in her pocket and sat on the edge of her bed. "You asked me about my birthday when you were here, maybe thinking it's a little strange that I don't remember the actual date for when I was born, but that's just one day to celebrate. I like marking the moment when something new begins. Like when I got married or became a mother or a grandmother. The day I die should be a celebration, too, because that will also be the start of something new. One of my favorite days is October 23rd, or as I like to call it—Fruit Crate Day. It's the day when Pastor Cooley found me on the church step. I always like to make an apple pie on that day."

"Well, this year we can celebrate the first time in twenty years that we get to spend Christmas together," Heidi said.

"We could call it Zeal Cooley Day."

"What do you mean?"

"When he found that letter in the fruit crate, my Mama asked that I would always know that I am loved—really loved, and you showing up on my doorstep a few months ago was an answer to his promise. When I lost your daddy and then your Poppy, it looked like I would be unloved, then you came back to visit…you helped Zeal Cooley keep his word."

"I'm so glad."

"Everybody needs kinfolk—blood relations or not, don't they? And I always had a family, even during those minutes on the church steps in that fruit create, when my mother was hiding in the bushes, I never was unloved. She was watching me just like Miriam watched baby Moses by the Nile River."

"What a sweet thought, Mo. I hope you're writing all of this down."

"I will. Don't you worry."

"So, are you going to eat turkey today?" asked Heidi.

"I'm going over to Pauline's. We're supposed to eat around one o'clock. Her husband Ray is trying his hand at a deep-fried turkey this year. Sounds a little silly to me. Why take something simple like roasting a turkey and throw in a mess of hot oil to make it dangerous. Pauline said they upped their homeowner's insurance just so he could do it. Anyhow, I told her I'd bring a banana cake, so I'd better hop to it."

"Okay. I love you."

"Love you, too, Doll Baby, from here to the hereafter and ten miles past that."

Morgan's Hat, Tennessee, 1941

Tillie waited until Thursday morning to deliver the news to Zeal about Alice's upcoming visit. She almost went over to his house as she was leaving the church office on Wednesday afternoon, but her female intuition was telling her that Zeal still wasn't ready to see the woman who had turned him down. Hers was a powerful ability which had rarely failed her, so Tillie listened to her little voice and vowed to speak to him the following morning.

Now that she was standing on his doorstep, she attempted to bolster her courage and fortitude before knocking. She was determined not to let his marriage proposal change their professional, working relationship.

"Good morning, Mrs. Bransford," Zeal said once he had opened the door. "The mornings are getting chilly now, aren't they? Come on in and have a cup of coffee, won't you?"

Tillie nodded and followed him into the kitchen. "I have news to share, Pastor," she said. She was watching him carefully, but he seemed his usual self; cheerful and cordial. She noted that his commonplace behavior struck her both as a relief and—she was embarrassed to admit to herself—a bit of an aggravation.

Zeal poured coffee into a cup which had been sitting upside-down in the sink drainer. "Do you take cream and sugar?" he asked.

"Just sugar, please."

They sat down in the living room with their steaming cups. "Moses is asleep in the crib. Thank the Lord, she's sleeping much better now. Her nights aren't nearly as fitful."

"Glad to hear it," Tillie replied and took a sip. "As to my news—I have found her—Moses' mother. Her name is Alice Mead, and she's the daughter of the late Olivia Simpson Mead." Tillie paused to let the shock of the news set in. "Miss Mead's a violinist playing with a touring orchestra currently staying in a hotel in Nashville. I've talked her into coming to visit Moses today. She's to come straight to the church, and then I'll bring her over here."

"I'm at a loss, Mrs. Bransford. I can't begin to think of how you've discovered the woman's identity and her whereabouts."

"I wish it were more impressive, but it came down to those recipe cards. Her name and the address of her music school were written on the back of one of them."

"Wasn't that fortunate? I'll be in prayer for her visit. Do you think she plans to take the baby away from here? That is, did she give you any indication of her plans?"

"Getting her to travel here is miracle enough for one day, I'd suspect," said Tillie.

"Wise words. We'll leave it to the Lord."

Tillie stood to take her cup to the sink. "I haven't had a chance to write your sermon yet, but I will get it done, quick as a wink."

"Well, I certainly appreciate you, Mrs. Bransford. I don't know what I'd do without your help."

"My pleasure, Pastor."

Tillie smiled as she left the pastorium. She always received such delight when delivering good news, but as she made her way over to the church office, she realized she was anxious about Alice's visit. Had she done the right thing telling Zeal? What if Alice didn't come, after all? Now he would know and be disappointed, but if she had waited to tell after Alice had arrived, Zeal might have wished for time to prepare himself. Such a dilemma!

Whenever she suffered from bouts of nervousness, Tillie felt better if she found something to clean. Her mother had been the same way. How many times had she seen the meek darling scrubbing the floor of their modest home once she had received bad news, usually something to do with her father's difficulty in keeping a job. Tillie could remember the scene clear as a bell—her mother scrubbing and singing hymns, stopping every so often to brush the hair from her face or massage her sore lower back.

Tillie wasn't interested in scrubbing the floor, but she could finish straightening Zeal's office. She attacked the stacks of books with renewed purpose until each one was in its rightful place. Then she returned to her own desk to work on Sunday's sermon. She was determined to get it to Zeal so that he could read over it, not wanting to have him repeat his unrehearsed performance from the week before.

Just as soon as she had placed her fingers on the keys of her typewriter, she heard a voice calling from the sanctuary. Tillie jumped up, accidentally stepping her foot in a wastepaper basket as she hurried to answer the call.

"Here!" Tillie shouted. "Come on back here!" As she smoothed her hair and adjusted her glasses, Tillie tried to calm the jittery feeling in her stomach.

A young woman stepped around the corner and stood in front of Tillie. She was tall and stylishly outfitted in a burgundy dress of soft velvet. A matching hat in the same shade of red was perched atop her black hair at a jaunty angle. She had a wool coat of black and red plaid draped across her shoulders. Tillie noticed a delicate-looking pin on the coat's lapel—a hummingbird, its body encrusted with tiny diamonds and wings made of rows of sapphires and garnets with a slender, gold beak. Tillie thought she looked just the women in her *Good Housekeeping* magazines. "You must be Miss Mead," said Tillie. "I am so glad you came."

"Please, call me Alice," she replied as she fidgeted with her gloves, looking around the room like she was expecting someone to jump out of a closet and yell, *Boo!*

"And you must call me Tillie." Tillie reached out to shake her hand, but instead of letting go, she held Alice's hand between hers and drew her closer. "Everything will be alright, honey. Let's go and see your baby."

They walked together to the pastorium and knocked on the door. As soon as Zeal let them inside, Alice ran to the fruit crate where Moses was lying, pulling on her own toes playfully. She picked up the baby and immediately began to sob.

"Sit down over here, Miss Mead," Zeal said as he led her to the sofa. "Let's all just get acquainted." He sat down next to Alice and handed her a handkerchief that Tillie noticed he had laid out on the arm of the sofa, probably in anticipation of this moment. "Mrs. Bransford, I made biscuits and brewed another pot of coffee for our visit. Would you mind bringing everything in here and setting it on that end table? I believe Miss Mead may require a hot drink after her trip."

Tillie carried a plate of biscuits and a little pot of strawberry jam into the living room. Then she went back to retrieve the coffee pot and cups. She didn't even try to look for the tray she had used to serve Zeal his eggs and toast when she had made his breakfast the week before, preferring to avoid bringing up any topics of caring for dead bodies on Alice's first visit. Tillie's intuition told her that the skittish young woman might bolt from the room if triggered by anything distressing or shocking.

Alice rocked back and forth with Moses in her arms while wiping her moist eyes and nose with the handkerchief. Zeal didn't speak. He stared at the tiny baby with his hands in his lap, waiting. Tillie ached to fill the silence, but she took her cue from Zeal and waited, too.

After several minutes of rocking and sniffing, Alice spoke, "I'm not a bad person. Truly, I'm not."

"I never once thought you were," Zeal answered softly.

"It's just that I don't have any family. I didn't know what to do."

"I've been a pastor for many, many years, and I've seen families through similar predicaments to yours. The difference is, though there was some embarrassment to how the child was conceived, in most instances there were relatives to step in and help. I feared you didn't have the aid of any close and caring kinfolk, so I hoped to give you an opportunity to change your mind, if you wanted to."

"But nothing is changed. I still can't take care of her and travel for my job," Alice said.

"We don't have to settle on any details just now," said Zeal. "It's about time for Moses to have another bottle. I'll go get it ready, and while you feed her, you can tell Mrs. Bransford and me all about you—where you're from and what you like to do. No one is asking anything else of you right now. Like Mrs. Bransford told me this morning, you being here is miracle enough for one day."

Zeal, Tillie, and Alice spent the remainder of the day chatting and eating biscuits and passing Moses around to be held and played with. Once it grew dark outside, Alice laid Moses back in the fruit crate and brushed the biscuits crumbs from her lap. "I'll have to hurry to catch the bus back to Nashville," she said, reluctantly.

"I'll drive you to the bus stop," Tillie replied from the kitchen where she was washing up the dishes.

Zeal walked Alice to the front door. "You are welcome to come back any time," he said. "And you think about what I said."

Alice glanced at Moses again before nodding her head and slipping out the door to stand on the dark porch.

Tillie had finished washing up the dishes and went to pick up her coat from the back of the armchair. Zeal reached it first and held it for her as she slid her arms into her sleeves. "Thank you for everything, Mrs. Bransford," he said. "God bless you."

Tillie saw that he looked drained and unsettled. She blushed at the realization that she suddenly wanted to stroke his whiskery cheek and tell him all would be well. Instead, Tillie focused on the task of putting on her gloves and said, "Good night, Pastor." Then she joined Alice on the porch and walked with her to the Plymouth parked in front of the church.

374 Verbena Drive

Pauline was watering the plants in Mo's bedroom when her cell phone rang. "This is Pauline Pendergrass, your Mary Kay beauty consultant. How can I help you find your beauty?"

"Hey, Pauline. This is Heidi. I tried Mo's phone, but she's not answering."

"Oh, hey, hon. Your granny is in the hospital. I'm so sorry I didn't call. She made me promise on a stack of Bibles that I wouldn't tell you about it."

"The hospital? What is it? What's wrong?"

"I came over here yesterday to help her put up a little tree—nothing big or fancy, just a little holiday cheerfulness for her front room. I could tell she was pretty tuckered out, so I came back to check on her last night, and I found her crumpled up on the floor of the den."

Heidi gasped. "She had collapsed? Was she responsive?"

"She could talk to me a little, but I called the ambulance right away. They're running tests on her and managing her pain."

"I'm supposed to fly there in a week—" Heidi began.

"If you can, I think you ought to come on now."

"You think she won't make it?"

"It looks to me like she'll be going on to her heavenly reward real soon, hon."

"Is she…I mean, can she talk?"

"Yes. She told me to come and water her plants, but it was difficult for her to get the words out. She's such a strong lady, but her body won't be able to bear much more of this." Pauline took a tissue from the box by Mo's bed and blew her nose. "This world is gonna lose an angel when she goes."

"I'm going to find the first flight that I can."

"Okay, hon. Let me know what you end up booking, and I'll send my Ray to come fetch you from the airport." Pauline looked out the window into the dark, swirling sky. "They're predicting record-breaking low temperatures and maybe snow—if you can believe what the weatherman on TV says seeing how most times he gets it wrong—but pack your warmest clothes just in case."

"Thank you, Pauline. I'll get back to you right away."

Morgan's Hat, Tennessee, 1941

Tillie had noticed that the can of Carnation milk for Moses' bottles was almost gone, so she stopped by Padgett's Grocery store to pick up another can on the way to the church office Friday morning. She knocked on the pastorium door to drop it off, along with a couple other sundry items and was greeted by Zeal in his overcoat and hat.

"Are you heading out, Pastor?" she asked.

"I was going to run over to Padgett's…" he began.

Tillie lifted the paper bag she was carrying. "I saw that you were running low on a few things—milk for the baby, sugar, coffee, oleo—and Mr. Padgett had a nice selection of ham hocks—I know how you like your pinto beans. Anyhow, I took the liberty of getting these and bringing them over so you wouldn't have to get out with Moses. She's liable to catch a chill today."

Zeal removed his hat, an old, plaid hunting cap with furry ear flaps which was so old that he had first started wearing it when he still had hair, and grasped it tightly in his hands. "If I didn't know you were such an upstanding Christian woman, I'd accuse you of sorcery! Your predilection for mind-reading is a wondrous thing, Mrs. Bransford!"

"I just had a feeling, that's all," Tillie answered.

"Well, come right in, and let me take that bag from you."

"No need, Pastor Cooley. I'll just put these away and head over to the office. I suspect that phone's been ringing and ringing these last few weeks without me there to answer it." Tillie set the bag on the

kitchen counter and removed the groceries, while Zeal took off his coat and hung it on one of the hooks by the door. Then he went to the bedroom and came back with a bundled-up Moses.

"Little Miss, we can stay indoors today, so you don't need this extra layer of winterwear," Zeal said while he gently pulled her arms out of the pale yellow knit cardigan which Moses was wearing on top of her gown.

From the kitchen, Tillie suddenly heard a clicking sound, like someone was tapping on the window. "What do you think is making that ruckus?" she asked as she reorganized a shelf of canned vegetables, turning each one so that their labels were more easily read.

Zeal picked up Moses and carried her to the front window, pulling back the curtains. A gray bird with brown striped wings and a rust-colored head was sitting on the sill, pecking his beak on the glass.

Tillie stepped over to the window to look at the bird. "My mother always said that a bird pecking on the window was bad luck. She said it might even foretell that someone would die soon."

"Someone dies every day, Mrs. Bransford, so that kind of prediction doesn't hold much weight with me. I think this little fella is pecking because he's looking for some seeds. He's trying to fatten up for the winter." Zeal walked over to the kitchen and came back with a small burlap sack of sunflower seeds. With Moses still in his arms, he carefully opened the door and tossed a handful of seeds onto the porch. Once he was back inside at the window, Zeal said, "That's a chipper sparrow. See its fine red cap, Moses? Watch it eat up those seeds. Oh yes, he's a hungry fella."

As Tillie watched the pair of them together, her heart swelled with powerful emotions. Ever since one particular discussion at a meeting of the Davis County League of Church Secretaries, Tillie had come to realize how much she had grown protective of her pastor. The other women in the group suggested that she try to distance herself from him, but she often found herself falling back to a position of worrying about him.

In the decades of being his secretary, Tillie had seen him by sick beds and marriage altars, always nurturing and wise, but she had never known his ability to care for something so small and fragile as a newborn. It was plain to see that he was a natural with Moses, and now she fretted that Zeal would struggle if Alice came back for the child. She agonized over the thought that she had once again contributed to his unhappiness.

Studying his tenderness with Moses, Tillie couldn't help but draw comparisons to the other men who loomed largely in her life—her unreliable father and her bullying husband. One virtue lacking in both men was gentleness, a quality many men would never aspire to but one which could alter the course of generations of families.

Tillie's thoughts were interrupted by Zeal's voice. She watched as he swung Moses side to side and sang to her:

> *Chippy, chip, chip. The sparrow sings a song.*
> *He wonders if you like his hat and if you'll sing along.*
> *He whistles to his lady bird to say his love is strong.*
> *He tells her that forever feels just like a day is long.*
> *Yes, forever with his darling sparrow flies by like birdsong.*

Once his song was finished, Tillie folded up the paper bag and left it on the counter. "I know just what I'm going to write about for your sermon, Pastor, so I'd better hop to it."

"Thank you, Mrs. Bransford."

"And I'll let you know the minute I hear from Miss Mead," Tillie shouted over her shoulder as she hurried out the door, anxious to get her thoughts on paper while they were fresh in her mind.

The startled sparrow flew from the porch and up to a neighboring pine tree where it chirped happily and settled onto a branch, its belly full of sunflower seeds.

Nashville Airport

Y*ou've reached the voicemail for Pauline Pendergrass, your Mary Kay beauty consultant. I want to help you find your beauty, so leave a message and I'll get right back to you.*

"Pauline? This is Heidi. I just landed. Call me." Heidi shifted the slipping strap from her bag back up to her shoulder. It had been more than a day since she had left L.A. Now she felt frustrated and un-showered and very worried.

She dialed Josh's number. "I made it," she said as soon as Josh answered. "I'm either going to get a ride to the hospital or rent a car. I'm just trying to decide which would be faster."

"I hate that I couldn't go with you," he said. "But I can fly there in a couple of days when we wrap up this rewrite."

"It's fine," Heidi said, trying to keep the irritation from her voice. "If it weren't for this stupid ice storm…" Heidi sprinted down the escalator, passing people and squeezing past their larger carry-on luggage.

"Take a breath. Sit down for minute. You sound like you're going to have a coronary."

"Sit down? Why would I sit down? I've been sitting for the past twenty-four hours. I've got to get to Mo." Her cell beeped in her ear. "Pauline is calling me. I'll talk to you later."

Heidi switched to Pauline's call. "Pauline, I'm here."

"Ray is on his way, hon. He'll find you at baggage claim." Her voice was shaky, and Heidi could hear her sniffing.

"I'm too late," Heidi declared. "Aren't I?"

"Oh, Heidi. Your granny is gone." Pauline fully gave herself to sobbing.

Heidi dropped into an empty seat, her phone still on but lying in her lap. She decided to give herself a minute, a full sixty seconds just to breathe in and out. Without wanting to, she imagined Mo lying on a grim hospital bed, still and ghostly—tubes and wires and a white sheet. Heidi closed her eyes and shook her head to dislodge the conjured image. Instead, she focused on remembering the meal she had shared with Mo on their last evening together before Heidi had flown to L.A. Over a slice of pineapple cake, Mo had told her that Pastor Cooley had taught all of the children in Sunday School to recite the Fruits of the Spirit to help them calm down. "It works better than counting to ten," Mo had told her. "Try it. I'll teach them to you if you don't know them."

Mo's voice seemed to be urging her again. *Try it.* "Love, joy, peace, patience, kindness, goodness, faithfulness, gentleness, self-control," Heidi whispered to herself. She inhaled, taking in as much air as she could until she thought she might pass out, before pushing her breath out slowly. Then she slipped her phone into her purse and followed the signs to baggage claim.

After a few minutes of waiting, a burly man in a bomber jacket approached her. "Heidi?" he asked. She nodded. "Pauline said she told you about your granny. So sorry for your loss, darlin'. This your only bag?" She nodded again. "You want me to take you to the hospital?"

"Yes," she barely choked out. "I need to go and say good-bye."

Morgan's Hat, Tennessee, 1941

Zeal received his sermon late Friday afternoon. Without waiting to speak to him, Tillie had knocked on the door and hustled away, leaving a bundle on his front porch—her usual typed sheets with the notecards paperclipped in the corner. Her action had left Zeal in a distraught mood all evening, but he assumed she was still embarrassed by his marriage proposal. He supposed he had botched the whole thing from start to finish. His wooing skills were rusty, but who would be surprised since the bachelor preacher hadn't confessed romantic feelings to a woman in more than thirty years.

Maybe it was the mention of the name, Olivia Simpson, which had stirred up so many feelings and planted in his head a renewed interest in the advantages of marriage. Each time he had come back to Morgan's Hat for visits while he was still in seminary, before he eventually took on his post at Berea Baptist, he had looked forward to calling on Olivia at the Lathrop Mansion. She was all sweetness with a quiet dignity and refinement, so different than the loud brood he had been accustomed to from his years growing up as the youngest of the large Cooley clan. On his last visit before graduating, he had hoped to propose, even going so far as to borrow money from his brother Mel—short for Melchizedek—to buy a ring. Walking to the Lathrop Mansion that day, Zeal had practiced what he would say, though he thought his proposal would come as no surprise. After all of the letters he had written her, surely Olivia would expect it. But when he had arrived, Miss Willadeene met him at the door and told him that Olivia had gone to Birmingham to get married. At first, Zeal had been devastated by the news. In all of their long, pleasant visits and written correspondence, Olivia had never mentioned the existence of a fiancé in Birmingham. He felt foolish, but his broken heart didn't prevent him from coming back to settle in Morgan's Hat.

Zeal thought about the photograph Olivia had given him and wondered where it was. He considered looking through the chest of drawers in his bedroom, but Moses was still sleeping, and he needed to study over his sermon once more before he woke her up and fed her.

Wearing his favorite cardigan and sitting in his most comfortable armchair with a cup of hot coffee on the end table, Zeal read through Tillie's words:

What do you want to do when you look up at the clouds? Stomp on them till they disappear? Lay down on them like a cozy mattress? Gather up handfuls and stick them in your pockets for later when you can enjoy their softness all by yourself?

Or what about a butterfly? Do you see it flying through the wildflowers and think it's an invitation to chase it down and capture it, or do you want to protect it? How you care for fragile things says a lot about who you are deep down inside.

Good men and women of Berea Baptist, if we aim to be like God and His Son Jesus, then we should set our minds to learning all the ways we are called to act. The Lord is just and longsuffering and mighty, but He is also gentle in His treatment of us. First Thessalonians 2:7 says, "But we were gentle among you, even as a nurse cherisheth her children." And from the Book of James we read, "For where envying and strife is, there is confusion and

every evil work. But the wisdom that is from above is first pure, then peaceable, gentle, and easy to be intreated, full of mercy and good fruits, without partiality, and without hypocrisy. And the fruit of righteousness is sown in peace of them that make peace."

Gentleness may be a thing we expect of our womenfolk, but the Lord asks us all to be gentle. All of us should be working towards peace, from the biggest foreman at the sawmill to the littlest child playing ball in the schoolyard, and gentleness gives us the frame of mind to encourage peace.

Zeal took a sip of his coffee and tried to concentrate on the passages of Scripture instead thinking about the way Tillie's sky-blue eyes were framed by her cheerful, purple eyeglasses or wondering how she got her waves of molasses-brown hair to stay piled on top of her head. Suddenly remembering his weak moment of wickedness, Zeal slid his hand in the pocket of his cardigan and pulled out the clip-on earring he had found on the floor by Tillie's desk. He gazed at it as if it were a priceless heirloom, then he sighed.

From the bedroom, Moses began to cry, so he set the earring by his coffee cup and went to change her diaper. "I'm coming, Little Miss," he called to her.

Once they arrived at the church, Tillie met Zeal and Moses at the door. "Good morning, Pastor," she said. "Can I take Moses for you? I'd be happy to hold her while you preach."

"Thank you, Mrs. Bransford." He passed Moses to her, and Tillie adjusted the baby's bonnet. "Did you have a chance to read over everything in the notes I left you?" she whispered.

"Yes," Zeal answered. "You did a marvelous job. Thank you again for your help."

Zeal vaguely noticed a frown pass over Tillie's face after he responded. He would've liked to question her about her reaction, but the organist was playing "Bringing in the Sheaves," and he needed to make his way to the pulpit.

As the song was ending and the parishioners resumed their seats, Zeal withdrew his sermon notecards from the inside pocket of his suitcoat. He flipped through them to check that they were in order—Tillie always wrote a tiny number in the corner of each of the cards, a habit she had begun after one especially windy Sunday in April when the sanctuary windows were opened and the cards flew from the pulpit and scattered, out of order, across the floor.

He hadn't looked at the cards yet, satisfied with the text of Tillie's typed-up sermon sheets. So when he saw three sentences, hand-written on the last card, Zeal squinted to read them. In her slanted, loopy script, Tillie had written: *You are the kindest, most gentle man I've ever known. I was afraid of all I would lose if I married again, but now I believe that gaining a family is worth whatever freedom I might give up. If you still want to, I will marry you.*

Zeal looked at the back of the sanctuary, searching for Tillie in her usual seat. He saw her there with tears in her eyes, sitting beside a young woman who was holding Moses and smiling. Alice had returned.

Zeal was dizzy with words and emotions, so much trying to burst out of him. He breathed through his nose and gripped the sides of the pulpit until his fingers hurt. When he finally regained his power of speech, he jubilantly exclaimed, "Good morning and welcome to the Lord's House at Berea Baptist church!" He put the notecards back in his coat pocket and continued. "I have a sermon here, but I believe I'll save it for next Sunday, if it's alright with you." The parishioners murmured a confused consent.

"Thank you." He took a deep breath. "You see, I have a story to tell you." Zeal opened his Bible, smoothing the pages affectionately. "There was a man named Daniel, a good man who was in a bad spot. He was in a pit, surrounded by hungry lions. And why was he there? Well, Daniel was facing those lions because he was caught praying to the Lord, just like he'd always done, but the king had outlawed that practice. Well, down in that pit, Daniel was frightened, but the Lord was nearby, watching this godly man fear for his life. So the Lord sent an angel. We don't know what that angel looked like. We might think he wore long white robes and a golden halo above his head and wings fluttering on his back. But angels can come in all forms, like the Good Book says, 'Be not forgetful to entertain strangers: for thereby some have entertained angels unawares.' Anyhow, Daniel prayed for help, and the Lord sent an angel who shut the mouths of those hungry lions. Such a miracle, brothers and sisters!"

Zeal was getting fired up now, his eyes bright and flashing. "You may be saying, 'Now, Pastor Cooley, that was long ago! The Lord doesn't perform miracles any longer.' But I tell you, He does! Miracles still happen! And I say that angels walk the earth, even now. They deliver good news like the multitude of heavenly hosts who sang to the shepherds about the birth of Baby Jesus on that hill outside Bethlehem. They minister to the needs of the weary and hungry like the angels who came to see to Christ after he was tempted by Satan in the wilderness. They remind us that God is with us, calling us mighty warriors even when we don't feel mighty, like the angel who spoke to Gideon by the winepress while he was hiding out from the Midianites. They chastise us when we need to hear tough words, like the angel who reprimanded Zechariah and took away his power of speech. And they shut out what frightens us, like the angel who came to sit in that dark, lonely pit with Daniel."

Zeal withdrew a handkerchief to wipe the sweat and tears from his forehead, eyes, and cheeks, while also giving him a brief moment to hide his face. He wanted to mask the intensity of his feelings from his congregation, at least for a little while. Zeal couldn't remember a time he had ever been happier, and he was anxious to share his joy with the three astonishing creatures sitting on the back row—the reasons for his miraculous happiness. When he felt that he could speak again, he finished his sermon.

"So I tell you that miracles still come to pass. Things you never thought you'd see—a healing, a changing, a persistence in the face of insurmountable trials and tribulations—these things still happen." Deciding that a short sermon could be just as useful as a long one and might actually supply another example of what his parishioners could list as a miracle, Zeal motioned for the congregation to stand after his abbreviated message. "Let's sing together, brothers and sisters!"

Once the organist began playing the first notes of "Love Lifted Me," Zeal dashed down the aisle to join Tillie, Alice, and Moses.

374 Verbena Drive

Heidi unlocked the door but stopped to stand on the threshold leading into Mo's house. From her position with her front in the warm house and her back still outside, she surveyed the living room, seeing all of the dated furniture and knick-knacks and framed pictures with a new awareness. Everything nearly vibrated with Mo's essence. Framed in the front window, she saw the little Christmas tree Pauline had set up for her grandmother. It was still resting on a card table covered with a green and red plaid tablecloth. Crocheted snowflakes, starched stiff and hanging on the branches, covered the tree, along with colorful, blinking lights. Everything was frozen in time, holding its breath from the time when Mo was last there.

"You okay?" Josh was standing behind her still on the porch. He rubbed his gloved hands together to stay warm.

"Yeah," she answered and walked the rest of the way into the room. "I just needed a minute."

Josh helped her take off her coat. While he was draping it over the back of the armchair, Heidi noticed a small wrapped package under the tree. She went to pick it up and saw her name written on the tag.

"Are you going to open it?" asked Josh.

Without answering, she slowly slipped off the ribbon and removed the paper. She opened the box and found a delicate brooch in the shape of a hummingbird. Covered in diamonds, garnets and sapphires, it had miniscule emerald eyes on either side of its head and a long, narrow golden beak.

"It's beautiful," Heidi said in a hushed, almost reverent whisper. She looked at the mirror by the front door and pinned the brooch on her sweater, smiling at her reflection.

"It looks vintage," said Josh. "Like something you'd see on an actress from an Alfred Hitchcock movie."

"I love it. I just wish I knew where it came from." Heidi walked into the kitchen and tossed the Elvis keychain on the counter. "Would you like a glass of iced tea?" she asked Josh.

"Sure," he answered. He followed her and sat down at the table. "If you think there is any..."

"Oh, I'm sure Mo has some." She opened the refrigerator and took out the pitcher. She heard herself refer to her grandmother in the present tense, as if Mo were just in the other room or out in the backyard, but she ignored her mistake, telling herself she would get to the reality of her situation eventually. "Thanks for driving to the house with me. I just couldn't bear to come in here alone."

"No problem." Josh smiled. "Hey, what was that last song we sang?" he asked. "The one with the pretty *come home* chorus."

"It's called 'Softly and Tenderly,'" Heidi responded as she sat down next to him, setting the glasses on the table. "The pastor said it was Mo's favorite. Apparently, she had the whole funeral planned out years ago."

"I wish more people could've come, but I guess the bad weather kept a lot of your grandmother's friends home."

"I'm so glad you didn't stay home," Heidi said. She reached for Josh's hand.

"Hey, I grew up in Michigan. A little ice isn't going to stop me."

"Well, it wasn't just a little ice, Tough Guy. Ray said there are parts of the city where lots of houses still don't have electricity. He said tons of trees came down and knocked out power lines. There are clean-up crews all over the place. It's a big mess."

"Were any of the trees on this property damaged?"

"I don't know," she answered. Heidi stood up, suddenly feeling anxious. "Oh, I hope Mo's weeping willow survived."

They grabbed their coats and went to the back door. As soon as she slid it open, the frigid wind was a brutal shock. It seemed to slap

Heidi's bare cheeks as it made her eye sockets feel like they were full of ice water. She instantly missed the warmth of Mo's house, but not just what flowed from the air vents. She missed the warmth of her grandmother's touch, like when she would reassuringly pat Heidi's arm or comb out and braid her wet hair.

Standing on the little concrete patio, Heidi realized that the cold air wasn't the only surprise. The moment she stepped into the backyard, she heard waves of humming and chattering, each individual sound was a coo or whistle. It was the thrumming sound of bird calls multiplied by a thousand. She turned to look at the weeping willow, the only tree still standing in Mo's backyard or the backyards of her nearby neighbors, and saw that the branches were packed with birdhouses varied by size and design, and each basket-like home was occupied by birds. Cardinals, blue jays, woodpeckers, chickadees, and sparrows had all found refuge from the storm in Mo's handiwork. Their songs filled the hollow stillness of the icy afternoon as they echoed off the frozen layer of snow on the ground.

Josh followed Heidi to the shed where she tore open the doors, staring at the empty space. "They're all up in the tree," she said mostly to herself. "But how?"

Josh turned on the light and walked into the shed to look around. In one dark corner, he found something box-like wrapped in an old pillowcase. He brought it out to show Heidi. "Maybe one of them didn't get hung up?" Josh speculated as he slid off the pillowcase, revealing an old fruit crate with the words PHARAOH ORCHARDS OF MEMPHIS written in faded red letters across the top. Inside the crate was a stack of spiral notebooks.

With shaking hands, Heidi took the top notebook off the stack and opened it to the first page. It read:

Dear Heidi,

I did what you asked me to do. I wrote down my memories. All of it belongs to you.

I love you from here to the hereafter and ten miles past that,

Mo

Mo's Story
Excerpt from Notebook #2

My mama came to Berea Baptist on important days. She came when she was young and visiting with Miss Willadeene so she could hear the sermon about the woman who bathed Jesus' feet with perfume. And she came on the Sunday morning when she decided to be my mother for good. Then she came again to be a witness at the wedding of Zeal and Tillie Cooley.

They didn't waste much time getting hitched after she said yes to his proposal. Sure, they had a few things to iron out, and one of them was making me and my Mama part of their family. After the wedding, we all moved into the pastorium. To hear Mama recall it, the people of Morgan's Hat accepted our situation pretty quickly. She said there were a handful of people who thought my mama's story was scandalous, but it shows how highly most everyone regarded the Pastor to see how they eventually just moved on and acted like she was their own daughter, and I was their granddaughter.

I grew up calling my grandparents "Lass" and "Pass." You see, she always called him Pastor and he always called her Lassie. Leastwise, that's what he called her at home in front of Mama and me. When he didn't think we were listening, he called her "My Sweeter Than Molasses Lass" on account of her waves of dark brown hair. Anyhow, apparently I just shortened their pet names for each other to give them new ones that I could say.

We all lived in that little house together for many years. My

Mama still played her violin in small concerts and even on a few recordings down in Nashville. She gave lessons to some of the kids in town, and they loved her teaching. She was so patient and a little shy. Her students just adored her for being so easy to please. I never was much of a musician myself, but Mama didn't seem to mind.

She was a meek woman, quiet and kind. Pass would say that she reminded him of her mother Olivia, on account of her graceful, refined ways. I used to love going in her closet to look at her fine dresses and elegant shoes. I would try them on and stand in front of her long, oval mirror with the gold-plated frame. She even had a little muff made of silver fox fur. I can remember clear as anything sliding my hands inside the muff and the feeling of its silk lining, so smooth against my fingers. Once, when I was six or seven, Mama came in and found me all dolled up in her things. I thought she might be cross, but she just went over to her bureau and took out her favorite hummingbird brooch and pinned it on me. She had the most beautiful smile.

Mama loved most any kind of music, and she would always have a song ready. No matter what we were doing, I could look at her and ask, "Mama, what song is in your head right now?" and she'd have an answer. Sometimes it was an old classical song without any words, so she would just hum it or sing the tune with *laaas* and *ooos*. Sometimes it would be a jingle she had heard on the radio advertising Pepsodent toothpaste or Alka Seltzer (*Plop, plop, fizz, fizz. Oh, what a relief it is!*). But her favorite were love songs like "Dream a Little Dream" and "Easy to Love" and "Someone to Watch Over Me." When I was little, she would pull me into her lap and sing them to me while we rocked in her rocking chair. Nothing felt safer than being wrapped up in her arms with my ear pressed against her chest, listening to her sing.

Mama never married or had any more kids, but I had plenty of kinfolk to grow up with, and most lived around us in neighboring counties. The Pastor had 17 older brothers and sisters. Their mama had taken their names from a Bible Dictionary. There was Amos, Beulah, Charity, Eden, and Fox (they all died before I was born). Next came Gilead, Hashbadana, Justice, Lazarus, and Melchizedek—but in the Cooley Family Bible they were listed as Gil, Hash, Jay, Russ, and Mel. Then there was a set of twins, Opal and Pearl. And finally the last six kids: Ransom, Seraphim, Toil, Wheat, Yoke, and Zeal. They all had bunches of kids who had bunches of kids. I don't get to see any of them much now. We mainly just send Christmas cards and catch up at funerals, but when I was young, I always looked forward to the Cooley family reunions! So much food and the best games!

Looking back on those days, I don't know that Mama enjoyed them as much as I did. It was kinda like she preferred to stay just on the outside of getting too awfully close to anyone other than me and Pass and Lass. Maybe it was a fear of getting hurt, or maybe it was shame or a guilty conscience, or maybe it was just her disposition. I'll never know for sure.

I was fifteen when the Pastor died. He had a heart attack while sitting in his favorite chair and reading his Bible, so it was the ideal way for him to go. Lass was still writing all his sermons for him right up to the Sunday before he died. Of course, she was heartbroken when he left us, but she handled everything perfectly. Lass asked Mama to play her violin for the service, choosing the hymn "Softly and Tenderly." One of the ladies from church sang it while Mama played. It was the most mournfully beautiful song I ever heard. After the funeral, I asked Lass why she picked such a song when we were already feeling so low. She said it was the Pastor's favorite hymn. She said that we're all weary at times, so it's a nice notion to think of Jesus watching and waiting and calling us to come on home.

We had them sing the same song at Mama's funeral, too. She lived just long enough to meet your daddy. As it turned out, she was sick and laid up as in the same hospital where I was giving birth. They wheeled me to her room after I had him, so that she could meet her new grandson. Her body was so full of tumors. The doctors told me they couldn't see how she was still alive, but I knew it was so she could hold little Phil. Sure enough, she died the next day. I was heartened to know that my sweet Mama had found peace at last.

When Mama passed, Lass sat down and wrote out what she wanted her funeral to be like. She was sure she'd go soon after, but she lived to be 102, still plugging away nearly twenty-five years after

Mama died. Lass asked to be laid out in her best white suit, the one she married Pastor in, with her purple beads around her neck. She even said what she wanted me to wear—something purple. The day she made her funeral plan was the day when she gave me her favorite grape earrings. Keeping with the theme, Lass said there should be purple flowers all around her casket—gladiolus and iris, salvia and hyacinth, wisteria and hydrangeas—all in different shades of purple. Of course, I did everything she asked me to do. The flowers were just gorgeous, and such a comforting sight to look at while I listened to the congregation sing "Softly and Tenderly" at the funeral of another beloved family member. At its best, that's what tradition can do for you—give you the expected when your world is turned upside-down and you can't make sense of how upset you are.

When you came to visit a few months ago, you asked me where I got my name from, and I guess I never got around to finishing that tale. You already know that Pass called me Moses because, in a manner of speaking, I was drawn from the Nile, but each of the parts of my whole name tell a little more of my story. For instance, my second name was a way for my mama to honor her mama, a woman she never got to know on account of her dying of TB just after Mama was born. When I was a girl, I was called Moses Olivia—or more like *Mosesolivia*, like it was all smooshed together into one word. It's a regular thing in the South for girls to go by two names. My third name was Mama's way of thanking her new parents. They made it all legal in the eyes of the court by fully adopting me. Then, of course, my last name is my claim to your daddy and Poppy. So my full name is Moses Olivia Cooley Seek. But for you, I wanted to be just Mo—short and easy to say and almost like Mom.

Each word of my name is like a stepping stone that explains my life. I was lost and found. I was unnamed and claimed. I was a tired and weary stranger, and then I gained a home.

Tillie's Favorite Recipes
from the Berea Baptist Cookbook

Eloise Hutton's Old Fashioned Tea Cakes

1 cup sugar
1 stick softened butter
1 egg
1 cup buttermilk
1 tsp baking soda
5 cups flour
1 tsp salt
1 tsp vanilla extract

Beat together sugar, butter, and egg. Add buttermilk and baking soda. Add flour and salt. Mix well and add vanilla.

Roll out ½" thick and cut with biscuit-cutter. Bake at 350-degrees until brown, about 15 minutes.

Lola Tharpe's Lemon Cheese Cake

1 (3 oz.) lemon Jell-o
1 cup boiling water
1 (8 oz.) cream cheese
½ cup sugar
1 tsp vanilla extract
1 (13 oz.) can Milnot or Carnation milk, whipped

3 cups graham cracker crumbs

½ cup melted butter or margarine

Dissolve Jell-o in water. Chill until slightly thickened. Cream together the cream cheese, sugar, and vanilla. Add Jell-o and blend well. Fold in stiffly whipped Milnot. In a separate bowl, mix together the graham cracker crumbs and melted butter. Pack 2/3 of the crumb mixture on the bottom and sides of 9x13 pan. Pour filling on the crust and sprinkle with remaining crumbs. Chill several hours or overnight. Cut into squares for serving.

Tillie Bransford's Chicken and Dumplings

3 lbs. chicken (whole or pieces)

1 small package chicken fat ("schmaltz")

Salt to taste

Yellow food coloring (optional)

1 stick butter, cubed

1 cup cold milk

Self-rising flour

Cook chicken with fat and water in large stewpot until tender. Salt (sparingly), to taste. Remove the cooked chicken to a plate and keep the broth simmering in the pot. Ladle out one cup of the broth and set aside for dumpling batter. Add a few drops of food coloring to broth.

Combine cooled broth, butter, and milk. Add enough self-rising flour until dough is thick enough to roll out. (Don't worry. You'll know it when you see it.) Roll on floured board and cut into strips. Drop strips into broth, but take your time. Don't crowd them. Add the shredded chicken back to the pot and serve.

Tabitha Langford Hoffman's Hawaiian Wedding Cake
Cake:
   2 cups PLAIN flour
   2 cups sugar
   1 tsp salt
   2 tsp soda
   2 eggs (WELL BEATEN)
   1 (20 oz) can crushed pineapple (DO NOT DRAIN)
   ½ cup Wesson oil
   1 tsp vanilla extract
  Stir well with a fork. DO NOT BLEND WITH A MIXER. Lightly grease and flour a 13x9 GLASS baking dish. Bake at 325-degrees for 40-45 minutes.
Icing:
   1 stick oleo
   1 (8 oz) package of cream cheese
   4 cups powdered sugar (MORE OR LESS DE-PENDING ON THE HUMIDITY)
   1 tsp vanilla extract
  Blend the margarine and cream cheese together and add sugar until the correct consistency is achieved. Add vanilla.
  Spread icing on cake WHEN IT COMES OUT OF THE OVEN. (If desired, sprinkle chopped pecans or shredded coconut on top of icing.)
  Note: This cake probably needs refrigeration after a day or so or sooner. It is a very moist cake and gets even moister later. IS BEST MADE THE DAY AHEAD.

Irene Marley's Railroad Pie
   1 lb. ground beef
   1 onion, chopped
   1 can tomato soup
   1 can water

1 can creamed corn
1 T chili pepper
1 batch of cornbread (following)
To make the cornbread topping, mix together:
1 cup flour
1 cup cornmeal
2 teaspoons baking powder
1/2 teaspoon baking soda
1/2 teaspoon salt
1 1/2 cup buttermilk
2 eggs, beaten

Brown meat and onions in a cast iron skillet. Drain the fat. Salt and pepper to taste. Mix in tomato soup, water, corn and chili powder.

Mix up cornbread batter. Spoon mixture over meat in skillet. Bake at 400-degrees for 30 minutes or until cornbread is done.

Mabel Jenkins' Banana Cake
1 ½ cups sugar
2/3 cup butter or shortening
1 cup mashed banana
2 eggs
1 cup buttermilk
1 tsp soda
2 cups cake flour
1 tsp vanilla extract

Cream sugar and butter. Add eggs and mashed bananas, beating more after each addition. Stir flour and soda together. Add flour/soda and buttermilk alternating between the two. Last, add the vanilla. Bake in two 9" cake pans.

Icing:
1 cup sugar

¼ tsp salt
½ tsp cream of tartar
2 unbeaten egg whites
3 T water

Mix ingredients together in a small saucepan. Cook for 5 minutes, beating with rotary beater the entire time. Remove from heat and add 1 tsp vanilla. Beat one more minute. This is enough icing to frost two cooled cakes.

Seraphim Cooley LaFevor's Brunswick Stew

1 ham bone
3 quarts of water
1 medium-sized chicken
A couple of sprigs of thyme
A few celery stalks, chopped
1 jar stewed tomatoes
1 onion, chopped
4 potatoes, peeled and cubed
2 cups butterbeans
2 cans corn, drained
1 cup catsup
salt to taste

Simmer the ham bone in a large cooking pot with water for 1 hour. Add the chicken to the pot. Add thyme, celery, and onions. Keep on simmering with no lid on the pot until the chicken is cooked. (This may take an hour or more.)

When the chicken is cooked, take it out of the pot and set it on a plate. Let it cool long enough so that you can handle it without burning your fingers. Tear it up into bite-sized pieces and put the cooked pieces back in the pot. Add the butterbeans, corn, potatoes, tomatoes, catsup, and salt (about a teaspoon should do).

If you like it with a bit of a kick, add some red pepper flakes or a few dashes of Tabasco sauce. Also, you may need to add more water if it gets too thick. Cook for about an hour, until the potatoes are fork-tender.

Marjorie Putnam's R.C. Cola Salad
   20 oz. can of crushed pineapples
   ½ cup water
   2 packages cherry Jell-o (3 oz. each)
   1 can cherry pie filling
   1 cup of RC Cola (minus a big swig)
Drain the pineapple but keep the juice. Heat up the pineapple juice and water to boil. Add Jell-O and stir. Stir in RC, cherry pie filling, and pineapple. Pour into greased gelatin mold and put in the refrigerator. After several hours, turn out your mold onto a plate. Serve cold.

Also by
Abby Rosser

Oh, to Grace

The Adventures of Dooley Creed
Believe
Hope
Remember

Also Available from
WordCrafts Press

White Squirrels...and other monsters
by Gerry Harlan Brown

Angela's Treasures
by Marian Rizzo

Land That I Love
by Gail Kittleson

Little Reminders of Who I Am
by Jeff S. Bray

www.wordcrafts.net

CPSIA information can be obtained
at www.ICGtesting.com
Printed in the USA
LVHW101743301221
707424LV00014B/446/J